DIRTY THERAPY (A MFM MENAGE ROMANCE)

TARA CRESCENT

My editor Jim takes the comma-filled words that emerge from my keyboard and shapes it into a story worth reading. As always, my undying gratitude.

Additional thanks for Miranda's laser-sharp eyes.

Cover Design by Kasmit Covers

FREE STORY OFFER

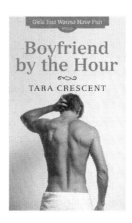

Sadie:

I can't believe I have the hots for an escort.

Cole Mitchell is ripped, bearded, sexy and dominant. When he moves next door to me, I find it impossible to resist sampling the wares.

But Cole's not a one-woman kind of guy, and I won't share.

Cole:

She thinks I'm an escort. I'm not.

I thought I'd do anything to sleep with Sadie. Then I realized I want more. I want Sadie. Forever.

I'm not the escort she thinks I am.

Now, I just have to make sure she never finds out.

DIRTY THERAPY

My O is missing. Two therapists are going to help me find it.

Two hours after Dennis proposes, I find my fiancé with his d*ck buried in Tiffany Slater's hoohah, and he has the nerve to suggest it's my fault.

Because I'm frigid.

Sure, I've never had an orgasm with him, or with anyone for that matter, but relationships are about more than good nookie. (Not that it was ever good. Adequate is more like it. Okay, who am I kidding? *Dennis couldn't find his way down there with a flashlight and a map.*)

Now I'm determined to find my missing O with the help of two of the hottest men I've ever set eyes on. Therapists Benjamin Long and Landon West. If these two men can't make me come, then no one can.

I shouldn't sleep with them. I shouldn't **succumb** to their sexy smiles. I shouldn't listen when their firm voices **promise** me all the pleasure I can handle.

I can't get enough. But when a bitter rival finds out about our forbidden relationship, *everything will come crashing down.*

1

MIA

I'm going to sum up the suckitude of my life with a three-point list.

1. Though I haven't had sex with my boyfriend for over a month, he proposed last night in an extremely crowded restaurant, and I said yes. Because everyone was looking at me and I didn't want to be the girl that broke his heart in a public setting. Even though I wasn't really sure I wanted to marry Dennis.

2. Once I got back home, I started thinking about whether we were doing the right thing. So, I went over to his place to talk to him, and I found him plowing his dick in Tiffany Slater's willing pussy. That wasn't good.

3. I started yelling. Instead of groveling, he yelled back. "You're frigid," he accused me. "I've never been able to make you come." Right. As if it's *my* fault that I have to draw him a map to my clitoris.

4. (Okay, I lied. This is a four-point list.) Worst of

all, when I threw his stupid engagement ring at his pasty-white butt, I missed. Big dramatic moment—ruined.

"So there you have it," I finish reciting last night's humiliating events to my best friend, Cassie, while unpacking a new shipment of cocktail dresses. "Can my life get any worse?"

It's eleven in the morning, or as I like to think of it, 'Treat Time.' Usually, this is my favorite part of the day. The store is quiet, and I can arrange the clothing neatly on hangers, organizing them by color and function. I can fiddle with the display cases of costume jewelry and make sure that everything is perfect.

Cassie, who runs the coffee shop next door, is my supplier of treats. She's watching me now, her eyes wide. "Dennis never made you come?" she asks, honing in unerringly to the most embarrassing part – the lack of orgasms. "Mia, the two of you dated for a year."

"I know."

She takes a bite of her muffin. Chocolate chip, if I know my friend. "Why on Earth did you keep going out with him?" she demands. Crumbs fall on my ornately tufted vintage velvet loveseat. Normally, I'd shoo her out of the way and bust out my hand-vac, but today's not a normal day. "The guy's not a looker, and he has the personality of a wet towel."

I feel strangely compelled to defend my ex-boyfriend, but then I remember Tiffany, and I clamp my mouth shut. "I tried to tell him what turned me on," I mutter, my cheeks flushed with humiliation. "At the start. He called me a pervert."

Cassie's eyebrow rises, and she gives me her 'what-the-

fuck' look. "He called you a pervert?" Her voice is dangerous. "And you still dated him after that?"

Worse, I almost married him.

I avoid Cassie's gaze. This situation would never happen
to my friend. She's bold and uninhibited, and she has every
guy in our small town wrapped around her finger. Me? I'm
the boring one in the corner, grateful for any scrap of attention that comes my way.

"Anyway." Cassie dismisses Dennis with a shrug of her
shoulder. "Forget Dennis. You dodged a bullet there. Let's
get you back on the horse. Friday night happy hour at The
Merry Cockatoo?"

Normally, even the mention of The Merry Cockatoo
would get a giggle out of me. The newly opened bar is on
the same block as my clothing boutique and Cassie's coffee
shop. My landlord, George Bollington, has been waging a
low-grade war with the woman who owns the bar, trying to
get Nina Templeton to change the name.

"We're a family-friendly town," he grouses every time he
sees me. "What kind of woman calls her bar that name?"
Mr. Bollington is so uptight he can't even say Cockatoo out
loud. Because I'm the town's resident good girl, he thinks
he's got a sympathetic audience in me. I get to hear him
grumble about Nina, about the sex therapists who've just
opened a practice in town, about people who chew gum and
listen to loud music, about people who litter... you name it,
and my landlord probably disapproves of it.

I agree with him on the litter, but the rest of it is Mr.
Bollington being a grouchy old man. Except for the sex therapists. That's professional jealousy. Mr. Bollington is a
psychiatrist, and he's grown accustomed to being the only
option in town. He now has competition, and he doesn't
like it.

Speaking of Mr. Bollington, the door bells chime, and my landlord walks in. When he sees Cassie sitting in my store, he frowns. Cassie is another person Mr. Bollington doesn't approve of. "Mia," he says, ignoring my friend, "I just saw your window display." His forehead creases with disapproval. "It's very unsuitable. This is a family-friendly town."

Last week, I'd received some incredible hand-made silk lingerie from a small French manufacturer. Each piece was so gorgeous that it should have been in a museum. I'd spent most of Saturday setting up a window display for the bras, panties, and slips. I should have known Mr. Bollington would get his knickers in a knot about it. (Ha ha. See what I did there?)

"Mr. Bollington, I run a clothing store." I try and keep my voice firm. "Window displays are an important part of my marketing strategy."

He's unmoved. "Need I remind you about the morality clause in your lease, young lady?" he demands. The threat is unmistakable. Take the offending display down, or my landlord will make trouble.

Cassie snorts into her muffin once he leaves. "One day," she gripes, "I wish you'd stand up to him and tell him his stupid morality clause isn't legally enforceable. You're going to take the lingerie down, aren't you?"

"Probably." I'm a people-pleaser. I want everyone to like me. And it seems easier to give in to Mr. Bollington's demands than fight him. It's just a window display, after all.

Cassie lets it go. "Back to more important things," she says. "Friday night. We'll get drinks, get tipsy, and go home with unsuitable men." She winks in my direction. "The kind that will have you screaming with pleasure. The sooner you forget about limp dick, the better."

I feel my cheeks heat. "Yeah, about that," I mumble. "Dennis might be right."

She frowns. "Right about what?"

Oh God. It's mortifying telling Cassie the truth. "I've never had an orgasm with a guy in my life."

Her mouth falls open. Thankfully, she's finished chewing her muffin. "With any guy?" she asks, her voice astonished.

I think back to the three men I've slept with. Brett, my high-school boyfriend, who I went out with for two weeks before he dumped me to date Gayla, a big-breasted blonde cheerleader. Tony, my college crush, who slept with me *once* before confessing that he preferred men. And of course, Dennis, who buried his cock in Tiffany's twat less than two hours after proposing to me. "Nope." I lower my voice. "There's something wrong with me, isn't there?"

"Apart from your horrible tastes in men, no." She gets to her feet and muffin crumbs cascade to the floor. "Friday. Meet me at six. Prepare to party your brains out."

Once she leaves, I stare blankly at the rack of beaded and glittering dresses and think about my ex-fiancé. Even at the beginning of our relationship, I'd never felt the kind of passion for him I read about in books. Maybe he's right. Maybe I am frigid.

Cassie isn't going to tell me the truth. The best-friend rules clearly state that she's supposed to say supportive things.

But there's another way to get the truth. As I vacuum up chocolate chip muffin residue, I make a decision. I'm not the kind of girl who sleeps with a guy she picked up at the bar. Even if I wanted to have sex with a stranger, they never tended to notice me. That kind of attention is reserved for Cass.

No, I'm going to solve my orgasm problem the responsible, adult way. I'm going to see a therapist. Not just any therapist. I'm going to see the sex therapists that Mr. Bollington hates. Benjamin Long and Landon West. Maybe they can figure out what's wrong with me.

2

BENJAMIN

I t's been two months since Landon and I opened our practice in this small town, and I can't say that I'm enjoying it so far. While the pace of life is a lot more peaceful than Manhattan, I'm used to the anonymity of the big city. In New Summit, everyone has their noses in our business all the time. Given what we do, that's a problem.

Landon, my partner and best friend, comes into my office at ten in the morning. "I need to talk to you about Amy," he says without preamble, taking a seat opposite me and propping his legs up on my desk.

I give him a pointed look, one that just makes him laugh. Landon knows I like my office tidy and organized, and he takes delight in messing with me. "Make yourself at home," I say dryly. I look him over. His hair is tousled, he hasn't shaved, and his eyes are red. "You look like hell by the way. Late night?"

He grins. "Samantha came over," he says. "She's a tiger, that one. She kept me up all night."

It's far too hard to keep up with Landon's dating habits,

but I could have sworn he was seeing someone else. "Weren't you sleeping with Claire?" I ask him.

"Not anymore," he replies with a shake of his head. "She was getting clingy. Talking about clingy, how's Becky?"

I gave him a puzzled look. "We broke up. Didn't I tell you?"

A faintly hurt expression flashes across his face. "No," he says. "You forgot to mention it. When did this happen?"

I do the math in my head. "Three weeks ago."

"Why did you break up with her? The two of you seem to get along well enough."

Landon knows me pretty well, so he's guessed, correctly, that I initiated the break-up. I think about the lawyer I dated for six months. Landon's right—Becky and I got along just fine. We never fought, we never argued, and we never even bickered. It had been an amicable, adult relationship, and it had bored me to tears.

"She wanted to move in," I explain.

Landon raises an eyebrow. "Let me guess," he says, his voice amused. "That suggestion filled you with horror. You thought about Becky's stuff all over your place, her toothbrush next to yours, her pretty lingerie in your closet, and you ran for your life."

"You don't need to psychoanalyze me," I tell him. Landon and I have been friends since college. He knows my flaws, and I know his. After a childhood filled with chaos, I'm almost pathological in my desire for calm. Landon's father cheated on his mother and slept around like a randy tomcat, and as a result, Landon avoids relationships, convinced he wouldn't be able to stay faithful. "I'm quite aware that I'm a little stuck in my ways."

"That's not what I was going to say," he replies, his expression serious. "I was going to tell you that you only pick women that you aren't truly attracted to, so it's easier to walk away from them when you're done."

I glare at my friend. That assessment is a little too close to the truth for comfort. "Didn't you say you wanted to talk about Amy? What has she done this time?"

Amy Cooke is our receptionist. She's new; the receptionist we had in Manhattan hadn't wanted to leave the city. She's still on probation, and at the rate she's going, she's not going to last very long.

"She outed Natalie to her sister-in-law." Landon's voice is angry. "Nat called me in tears this morning. It seems that Amy ran into Doris in church, and proceeded to ask her if Nat's husband knew what she did in our office."

I see red. Our practice specializes in sex therapy, and Natalie is one of our best surrogates. We use her to help clients who are having issues with their sex lives.

Unfortunately, surrogacy is still considered similar to sex work, and while Natalie's husband knows what she does for a living, the couple would prefer that no one else does.

Now Amy has outed Natalie to her family.

"We should fire her," I say flatly. "Amy knows how important confidentiality is. If she can't respect the most basic rules of our profession..."

Landon winces. He's kinder than I am. "Give her a warning," he says. "Tell her that she's out of second chances."

I frown. "You do it then," I tell him. "I'm too angry."

"Not a chance," he says promptly. "She has a crush on me. She'd be more terrified if you yell at her."

"Fine." Amy has to realize how important discretion is in our profession. Otherwise, she is going to get herself fired. Already George Bollington, the psychotherapist in town, is gunning for us. We don't need any more hassle.

My intercom buzzes just then. "Dr. Long? Dr. West?"

Amy's voice sounds in my office. "Your ten thirty appointment is here. Mia Gardner."

"Thanks Amy." I put the phone on mute and grin at Landon. "I hope you're ready to put your thinking cap on."

"New patient?" he asks. Landon and I see new patients together, at least until we have a treatment plan in place. "Let's go."

3

LANDON

There's only one word I can use to describe the woman who waits in my office. *Hot.*

She's in her mid-twenties. Her eyes glitter like green emeralds. Her hair is dark and lustrous, cascading in long, loose waves down her shoulders. Her body is the kind that a man dreams of, curvy and lush.

Except she's a prospective client, for fuck's sake. And though Ben jokes that I'll screw everything in a skirt, I have some boundaries. Clients are always off-limits.

"Ms. Gardner," I greet her with my most professional smile. "I'm Dr. West. This is Dr. Long. Please, sit down."

I wave toward the deep burgundy couch, and she perches on the very edge of it. Her fingers are clenched into fists, and she's yet to say a word.

"What brought you in today, Ms. Gardner?" Ben asks encouragingly.

She bites her lower lip. My cock takes note of the way her teeth indent the flesh, and I stir in my armchair, trying discreetly to adjust myself. God, this is embarrassing. I'm a sex therapist. I've watched people get fucked in this office, and I've never yet had to fight off an erection.

Fuck me. My dick hardens even further at the thought of seeing Mia Gardner naked.

Okay. Focus, Landon. She's here for help.

"Ms. Gardner." I lean forward. "It's okay. You can tell us what the matter is. Everything you say in this office is confidential. We're here to help."

She nods. "I have a problem," she says, her face flushed. Her voice is barely a whisper. "I don't think I enjoy sex."

"Why do you think that?" Ben asks her.

Her eyes drop to her lap. "I never orgasm," she mumbles. "My fiancé thought I was frigid."

She has a fiancé? I don't know why that bothers me as much as it does.

Ben is more helpful than I am. "It's pretty common not to orgasm with a partner."

"It's not just Dennis," she confesses, her hands worrying the fabric of her skirt. "I've never been able to come with any partner."

"Couples sometimes fall into a rut," I suggest. "They find it helpful to tell each other about their fantasies. Role play, kink. Whatever jolts you out of your rhythm."

Her face turns fiery. "Have you tried telling him what turns you on?" I continue.

"What turns you on, Ms. Gardner?" Ben's voice drops an octave, and his eyes glitter with heat. Whoa. Benjamin Long is interested in this girl too. Well, well.

"It's too embarrassing." She can't look at us.

"If you don't tell us, we can't help you."

"I just can't," she wails.

I have a brainwave, which is a miracle, given that most of

my blood has pooled in my dick. "Sometimes, when our clients are having trouble relaxing, we use hypnosis."

"Good idea, Dr. West," Ben says, giving me a sidelong look. He turns back to Mia. "Would you like to try that?"

She bites her lower lip again. I can see her debate it in her head.

"We record the session," I assure her. "So you don't have to worry about what you say."

She appears to reach a conclusion. "Yes," she nods. "I really want to solve this problem of mine, and if that's what it takes, let's do it."

Ben's the hypnotist. "Lie back on the couch," he instructs Mia, while I set up the recorder.

She gulps, but obeys. She stretches out on the red burgundy velvet, her skirt riding up to mid-thigh. Her skin looks creamy and soft and very touchable.

"You have nothing to worry about," Ben assures her. "Despite what you hear, we can't make you do anything during hypnosis that you won't do otherwise. It's just to get you to calm down."

He looks deep in her eyes, the lucky dog. "Relax," he says, his voice low and soothing. "Let your muscles sink into the couch." He draws out his sentences, the syllables slow and smooth. "Breathe in. Fill your chest and lungs with air."

She complies, and her breasts strain against her shirt. I want to adjust myself but can't. Until Mia goes under, sudden movements will startle her and pull her out of her trance.

"Good," Ben continues. "Now breathe out slowly. Empty your lungs."

After several steadying breaths, Ben proceeds to the next step. Despite what you see in pop culture, you don't need a swinging watch to hypnotize someone. Just a focal object.

Unfortunately, Ben picks me. "I want you to look at Dr. West's face," he instructs. "Focus on him. Don't move your eyes away from Landon, Mia."

Her pretty green eyes meet mine. There's a hint of nervousness there, but as Ben goes through each step, it disappears. After five minutes of slow, patient encouragement, her eyes grow heavy, and her breathing evens out.

Ben nods at me. She's good to go.

"We were talking about sex, Mia," I say. "Tell us what you want."

"Dennis was tentative," she murmurs, her voice soft. "Sometimes, I wanted him to take charge."

"Take charge how?"

She hesitates. "I wanted him to push me against a wall," she whispers. "Pull my hands above my head and hold them in place. I wanted him to be forceful. I wanted to be taken."

Stay calm, Landon.

"What else?" My voice is strained. "What do you fantasize about?"

"I want to be spanked," she replies. "I want to be dragged over a man's lap." Her expression turns dreamy. "He'll pull my panties down, and he'll order me to take my punishment like a good girl. And if I don't obey, he'll tie my wrists up so I can't move."

Oh my fucking God.

Even hypnotized, her cheeks go pink. "Then, once the spanking is over, he'll push me down on my knees, and he'll thrust his cock into my mouth."

Ben makes a strangled noise in his throat. Thankfully, it doesn't stop Mia Gardner, because she keeps talking. "Sometimes," she whispers, "I even dream about more than one cock. One in my pussy, one in my ass. Taking me hard."

This girl will be the death of us. Her fantasies are dirty and kinky, and I want to fulfill them.

She's a prospective client, asswipe. Keep your dick in your pants.

Ben's heard enough. He pulls Mia Gardner out of her hypnotic trance. When she's sitting on the couch again, her back straight, her hands clenched in her lap, he continues gently. "Do you remember what you told us you want?" he asks her.

She shakes her head.

I swallow. Mia is an irresistible combination of good-girl on the outside, and hot kinky vixen when her inhibitions are down. Following procedure, I copy the recording on a flash drive and give it to her. "If you want to listen to it later," I say in explanation.

Ben takes a deep breath to steady himself. "It sounds like you want to spice up your sex life," he says. "Perhaps your orgasm problems are tied to that. Have you tried talking to your fiancé?"

Her fiancé. What a douchebag that guy must be. If I had a woman like Mia in my bed, I'd make damn sure I please her.

Ben says *tied*, and I think of Mia stretched out on the couch, her arms above her head, bound together with a tie. Not mine; I never wear one. Ben's tie would work nicely, though.

"I can't. We broke up."

An unexpected surge of triumph runs through my blood. Yes. She's single. *Tell me more about your fantasies,* I want to urge. Ben and I have shared women in the past. We haven't done something like that in a long time, but for this woman, I'll be happy to make an exception.

"We have some other options," Ben says. "If you'd like,

we can explore using sexual surrogates to help you climax during sex."

She sits up. "A surrogate? You mean someone will have sex with me while you watch?"

"We're trained professionals," I reply. "I know it sounds awkward, but it isn't as bad as it sounds."

She jumps to her feet, her palms pressed against her cheeks. "I can't," she says, her eyes wild. "What was I thinking? Oh my God, I need to get out of here."

She rushes out of my office. I stare after her retreating back. "Well, that went well," Ben mutters. "Now I get to go and yell at Amy. What a fucking day."

4

MIA

Shrinks are not supposed to be this good looking. They're supposed to be pudgy and balding, not smoking hot.

Dr. Landon West and Dr. Benjamin Long clearly didn't get that memo.

Holy smokes. I think I almost had a heart attack when they walked into the office. When Dr. Long told me to lie back on the couch, I was seconds from coming. Listening to his deep voice, looking into his chocolate brown eyes, feeling his warm smile wash over me... *shit*. Even now, thinking about him makes me ache between my legs.

Then there's Dr. West. Dark hair, stubble covering his face, wide shoulders, and if I'm not mistaken, I caught a hint of ink under his shirt sleeves. Landon's a bad boy, through and through. He's like catnip for a good girl like me.

There was a wicked glint in Dr. West's eyes when he looked at me at the end of the session as if what I said had surprised him. He'd been hard when he handed me the recording; I'd caught a glimpse of his cock tenting his slacks.

They want to watch a stranger make me come.

I gulp. When they'd said that to me, a pulse of pure lust had shot through my body, and I'd imagined them joining in. I'd imagined Ben's big palm kneading my breasts. Landon's strong arms pushing my knees apart and finding my pussy soaked.

Then I'd come to my senses. Good girls don't go to sex therapists. What was I even thinking? Dennis was right. I am a pervert.

Speaking of which, it's making me nervous that I can't recollect what I told them. With shaking fingers, I turn on my laptop and plug in the USB key Landon gave me.

Lie back on the couch.

Hearing Dr. Long's voice, my hand slips between my legs. I'm soaked. My panties are wet, my pussy slick with desire.

What turns you on, Mia? What do you fantasize about?

Landon West's voice is deep. Silky smooth. I close my eyes and lean back on my futon. Spreading my thighs, I hone in on my clitoris, tracing small circles around the erect nub.

Dennis was tentative, I hear myself say. *Sometimes, I wanted him to take charge.*

My cheeks flame. I can't believe I actually said that.

Though I'm mortified, I'm still touching myself. I press down on my clit, harder than before. Closing my eyes, I imagine doing this in front of the two doctors. They wouldn't be timid. They'd be forceful and dominant. They'd order me to spread my legs wider. They'd command me to get naked.

In almost a trance, I slip my panties off. I pull my breasts out of my bra cups, and my thumb grazes at my nipples until they are hard with desire. I pinch them between my fingertips, groaning at the pleasurable pain that radiates from my breasts to the rest of my body.

I want to be spanked, Hypnotized-Mia says. *I want to be dragged over a man's lap.*

Wait, what? I said that to them? No wonder they looked at me weirdly.

I rub faster, my ass grinding into the futon, my fingers pulling at my nipples feverishly. My entire body tightens and clenches, and a familiar pressure fills me. No guy has ever been able to get me off, but I'm an expert at making myself come. I've had lots of practice. I can go from zero to sixty in less than five seconds. Ferrari has nothing on me.

Sometimes, Nympho-Mia says softly, *I even dream about more than one cock. One in my pussy, one in my ass. Taking me hard.*

That's all it takes. I hear my deepest, darkest fantasies voiced aloud, and it's enough to push me over the edge. My muscles quiver and spasm, and my body floods with pleasure.

When I regain the ability to think, I feel awful. I'm no closer to finding a solution to my orgasm woes and worse, Dr. Long and Dr. West, two of the hottest men I've seen in a long time, probably think I'm a dirty slut.

BENJAMIN

I'm not going to lie. I'm glad Mia ran out of our office.

Landon and I have been working together for over a decade. I can honestly say that we've never, in that time, been attracted to a patient. It would be a huge violation of our professional ethics.

But in that room, listening to Mia Gardner confess she fantasizes about a cock in her pussy and a cock in her ass, I almost blew my load. As did Landon.

Thank heavens she's not a client. I don't think I could stand the idea of one of our surrogates touching Mia. I want to reserve that particular pleasure for myself.

Okay, I'll share with Landon. He is my best friend, after all. But no one else.

Pushing my inappropriate thoughts of Mia Gardner out of my head, I walk to the small reception area. Amy's sitting there, fiddling with her cell phone. "I need to talk to you," I say bluntly. "Did you tell Doris Thorpe that Natalie works as a surrogate for us?"

Her furtive expression gives her away. "I just asked Doris

what she thought of Natalie's new job," she mumbles. "How was I to know that it was a secret?"

Bullshit. Amy can try to spin this any which way she wants, but the truth is, she's a gossip. She had no business discussing Natalie. The rules are pretty clear. "Let's go over this again." Fucking Landon is a softie with a heart of gold and Amy's given him some sob story about how she's been out of work for six months and how much she needs this job. Given her situation, you'd think she'd be a bit more discreet.

"Speaking of which, I can't believe Mia Gardner came to see you." Her eyes are round with curiosity. "What's wrong with her?"

The thought of Mia being the subject of Amy's gossip makes me see red. "None of your fucking business," I snap.

Her expression turns righteous. "You can't talk to me like that," she says sullenly.

I inwardly berate myself for losing my temper. I pride myself on staying calm, no matter what the situation. Control is power. "Amy," I say, glaring at my receptionist, "You outed Natalie to her family, and that's unacceptable. You've repeatedly been warned about confidentiality. Consider this your last warning. If you can't keep your mouth shut, I suggest you seek employment elsewhere." Cool down, Ben. "Have I made myself clear?"

She doesn't meet my eyes. "Yes, Dr. Long."

Back in my office, I shake my head. I regret the day we hired Amy. She came highly recommended by the only other psychotherapist in town, Dr. George Bollington. But since then, I've learned that Bollington thinks that sex therapy is just another word for prostitution. And while Amy is familiar with insurance forms and the myriad other bits of paperwork that comes with running a doctor's office, she's a gossipy bitch who loves poking her nose in things that don't concern her.

God, I miss New York.

Still, the move's been good for Sophia. In Manhattan, Landon's teenage sister had surrounded herself with a group of troublemakers and seemed intent on spending her time partying and doing drugs. In New Summit, away from bad influences, she's settling down and finally paying attention to her schoolwork again. That's worth any amount of bullshit.

LANDON

Friday morning, Sophia and I are eating breakfast when she looks up. "Is it okay with you if I get a job after school?" she asks me.

Well, this is a pleasant change.

I've been Sophia's guardian for the last four years since our parents died in a car crash. Our relationship has been rocky at times; Sophia was devastated when our parents were killed, and I had no idea how to parent a teenager. Things are slowly getting better.

Sophia's friends in New Summit all have part-time jobs. I guess she wants to be just like them. It's a vast improvement over getting busted for underage drinking.

"Where?" I ask my sister.

"There's a bar in the downtown area called the Merry Cockatoo," Sophia says. "They're hiring line cooks and servers."

"A bar?" I stiffen in disapproval. "I don't think so, Sophia."

I brace myself for a tantrum. Sophia surprises me. "I thought you'd react that way," she says, "but I won't be working the floor. I want to be a line cook. Nina, the woman who owns the bar, has an amazing menu, and I want to become a chef."

"You do?" This is the first time Sophia's expressed any interest in a career. "I didn't know that."

She rolls her eyes. "Landon, I do most of the shopping around here. I do all of the cooking. You really haven't noticed?"

I grin at my sister's irritated tone. "Okay, tell you what, I'll check out this bar and talk to the owner. If it seems on the up and up, you can work there, okay?"

"Yes." She jumps to her feet and hugs me. "Thanks, Landon. Will you go tonight? Nina said she'd be at the Merry Cockatoo all night long."

"Sure." Ben and I have been too busy setting up our practice to check out New Summit's nightlife. Might as well rectify that tonight.

MIA

The Merry Cockatoo is packed with people. Cassie and I fight through the crowd, trying to reach the bar. Nina Templeton is behind the counter, helping her staff out by pouring beer. "Mia, Cassie," she yells when she sees us. Nina has only one volume—loud. "It's so great to see you."

"And you," Cassie shouts back. "You're busy tonight."

Nina gives us a thumbs-up. "I know, I love it. I'm hiring again. You ladies know someone who's looking for a job?"

We shake our heads. Without asking, Nina pours me a small taste of an IPA. "It just came in," she says. "Nice, right?"

I nod appreciatively, and the four guys standing next to us at the bar give me a strange look. "Chicks don't normally drink beer," one of them says. He's wearing a t-shirt that says 'Blink if you want me.' Classy.

Nina pushes a pint of the beer in my direction. Cassie, who never met a craft beer she liked, opts for a glass of white wine. "Are you ready to mix and mingle?" she says to me, looking around the room with an assessing eye. "See anyone hot?"

She says hot, and a mental image of Dr. Long and Dr. West flashes in front of my eyes. All week, I've been jilling off to that damn recording, and it's only made me hornier. I've barely thought about Dennis. He's tried to call me more than twenty times, but I've ignored every single one of his phone calls and texts. He's a cheating douchebag, and I want nothing to do with him.

"Not really." The guys next to us have heard Cassie, and are giving us creepy looks. I grab my friend by the sleeve and inch her away from them, pulling us to a corner.

"What gives?" Cassie asks me with a frown.

"I was getting asshole vibes off those guys," I tell her.

She looks at them, and an expression of disgust fills her face as she reads the frat-boy slogans on their t-shirts. "FBI. Female Body Inspector. Seriously, if you want to get laid, why would you wear that idiotic shirt? I'm not sure what I'm more offended by, the sexism or the stupidity."

I grin at her indignant face. "Drink up. You promised me a night of partying, and I'm going to hold you to it."

Three hours later, I'm well and truly shit-faced. "Nina," I scream, placing my elbows on the wooden bar to steady myself, "I need a refill."

Nina raises an eyebrow. "Are you sure there, *drinky*?" she asks me. "These IPAs pack a punch, and you've already had five pints."

"I'm sure," I slur.

Cassie gives me an indulgent grin. "Yeah, she's had a rough week, Neen," she says to the bar owner. "She broke up with Dennis."

"Because his dick was in Tiffany Slater's hoohah," I

announce to the room. "Twatwaffle." That word sounds funny when I say it, so I say it again, louder. "Twatwaffle."

Several people look up at that. "Ahem," Cassie says. "Maybe this isn't a good idea, Mia. We should probably call it a night."

"Nah-uh." I glare at my friend. The room's spinning about, and deep down, there's a voice that tells me that she's probably right. I should go home. "You promised me a fun evening out," I pout. "Plus, you said I could go home with an unsuitable man."

"An unsuitable man?" A male voice cuts in, sounding amused. "Is that your goal for tonight, Ms. Gardner?"

I look up. Standing next to me is Landon West, and behind him is Benjamin Long. I feel myself blush. I'm about to say something, but my tongue feels woolen and odd. I sway on my feet, feeling woozy.

I start to collapse against his broad chest. Right before I pass out, his arms go around me. All I can think is, this feels really good.

BENJAMIN

We walk into the Merry Cockatoo, and the first woman I see is Mia Gardner. She's sitting at the bar, wearing a short floral skirt and a silk navy blue tank-top. The skirt rides up her thighs, showing long expanses of creamy skin.

God, she's beautiful.

And, judging by the way she's clinging to the counter, she's drunk.

She's slouched in her barstool, laughing and saying something to the woman next to her. Twatwaffle, she screams, collapsing in giggles. The bartender pours them both a drink with a grin and a roll of her eyes.

That's when I see it. There's a group of guys standing next to Mia and her friend, and one of them slips a roofie into their drinks. Nobody notices. Mia's friend practically gulps down her glass of wine. Mia takes a slower sip, and half her beer dribbles down her top. A wet stain spreads over her shirt, and her nipples poke out under the silk.

I nudge Landon and gesture to Mia. From the way his

mouth's hanging open, he's noticed her too. "She just got roofied by those assholes," I tell him grimly.

His eyes go wide with surprise. "Let's go kick their asses," he snarls.

I place a hand on his arm. "Let's not," I suggest. "We can't risk a scene. Bollington's waiting for us to put a toe out of line so he can report us to the Association. Let's just get Mia out of here."

Landon doesn't like my suggestion, but he recognizes the wisdom of my words. This is a small town, and we have to fit in. Landon can't afford to uproot Sophia; she's just getting settled into her school. "Fine," he says reluctantly.

We march up to the bar. "These assholes just slipped something in these drinks," I say to the woman behind the bar. "What kind of place are you running here?"

She inhales sharply. "They did?" She signals to the bouncer, then gives us a searching look. "You're the psychologists, aren't you? The ones who just moved into town?"

Ah, the advantages of living in a small town. Everyone knows everyone else. "We are, yes." I nod. Landon's saying something to Mia, who's swaying on her feet and slumping against him. "We are, yes."

"I'm Nina Templeton," she says. "I own the Merry Cockatoo. Listen, can you get Cassie and Mia home? I can't leave here, and I want to make sure they're safe."

Cassie must be Mia's friend. She speaks for the first time. "Mia's right," she chuckles. "You are hot." She winks at us. "Hot," she repeats. "Hot, hot, and hotter."

Drunk as skunks, both of them.

A shard of worry pierces me. Roofies mixed with alcohol is a dangerous combination. In extreme cases, Mia and Cassie could go into a coma. Someone needs to watch over them, just in case they need to be rushed to the emergency room. "How many drinks have they had?" I ask Nina.

She frowns. "Mia had five," she says. "Cassie had four, I think."

Shit. "Do they live alone?"

"Cassie lives with her sister just outside town," she replies. "Mia lives alone above her shop."

"Okay." I nod at Landon. "Let's take these ladies home."

Cassie's sister, Kelli, is a nurse. "I'll watch her," she says when we explain the situation. "I know the symptoms. I'll drive her to the ER if she doesn't wake up in a few hours. Do you want me to watch Mia as well?"

Cassie's stumbling around the living room, giggling as she collides against the coffee table. A pair of iron candlesticks falls to the floor with a loud clang. Kelli grimaces as she surveys her sister.

"No," I reply. Kelli has her hands full already. I'm not letting Mia out of my sight. "We'll take her home."

"Okay," she agrees at once. "Thank you so much for bringing Cassie home. I hope those guys get arrested for what they did."

Forget getting arrested. They deserve to get their faces punched in. Hopefully, Nina Templeton's bouncer is teaching them a lesson about drugging innocent women right now.

Back in the car, Mia's slumped in the back seat, leaning against Landon's shoulder. I exchange worried glances with him. "I don't know where her house is, do you?" I ask him.

He shakes his head. "Mia," he shakes her gently. "Sweetie, what's your address?"

She doesn't hear him. "Hey, it's Dr. Long," she says, her eyes wide. Her hands move ten inches apart. "How long is Dr. Long?" She giggles at her joke, and then she runs her hands over Landon's thighs. "How west is Dr. West? Oh wait, that doesn't make any sense." She giggles again.

Landon's cock hardens. "What?" he asks me defensively, as I look at him with a raised eyebrow. "I'm not going to do anything, but come on, Ben. I'm only human, and she's really hot."

"Who's hot?" Mia's fingers stroke Landon's bulging erection, her expression filled with lust. "Whoa there. That's a big dick."

"Ben, for heaven's sake." Landon moves Mia's hands away and gives me a frustrated look. "Let's get her to bed before I do something I regret."

"Fine."

I drive toward my house, more than a little envious of Landon. Thankfully, there's no traffic on the streets, because I'm distracted by the sight of her running her hands all over Landon's body. To his credit, Landon tries to stop her, but she's drunk, and she's determined.

In twenty minutes, I pull up in front of the Victorian manor that I bought last year. Landon gets out, and the two of us help Mia to her feet. She stumbles as she moves, and her eyes keep shutting. The Rohypnol is starting to take effect. She's going to be out for hours.

We help her to a guest bedroom. "My shirt is wet," she slurs, sitting on the edge of the bed. Before we can stop her, she tugs the garment over her shoulders, and her bra-clad breasts come into view.

God, she's gorgeous. I should avert my eyes; she's absolutely out of it. Tomorrow morning, she's going to be mortified when she remembers this evening.

Except I can't tear my eyes away from those creamy, luscious breasts. And when she fumbles with her bra clasp and peels the lacy garment off, I can't stop staring at her deep rose nipples, erect and needy.

I want to taste her. I want to suck those hard nubs between my lips. Nibble at her tender flesh and hear her moan as she responds to my touch…

"Ahem." Landon clears his throat and adjusts himself discreetly. "Mia, take off your shoes, honey."

"I can't." She looks sad, her lips turning downward as she wriggles her foot. "It won't come off."

My lips curl up into a grin. Mia's wearing strappy sandals. I get onto my knees and unbuckle them, unable to resist running my fingers up her soft calves as I do so. Landon gives me a dry look. "Ben, for the love of God, we need to get out of here."

He's right. I slide Mia's shoes off her feet and back away. "Go to bed," I tell her.

"Alone?" Her face scrunches into an adorable pout. She thrusts her breasts forward. "Don't you want me?"

"Mia, honey, you're drunk, and you've been drugged," Landon says gently. "You need to sleep this off."

"Dennis didn't want me either," she says despondently. "Nobody wants me. I'm the boring good girl."

"I want you." My voice comes out harsher than I intended. "Landon wants you. But not like this." God, if only she were sober, I'd be on her like a rabid dog in heat.

But she's not. I turn on a lamp by the side of the bed and turn off the overhead light. "We'll keep checking in on you," I tell her. "Go to sleep."

This is going to be a very long night.

9

MIA

I wake up in a strange bedroom.

Sunlight streams in through a wide bay window. A couch is tucked into the recess, creating a comfortable nook to take advantage of the view. Cream and taupe pillows accent the couch, and the room looks warm and inviting.

I sit up on the bed, and the soft sheet covering me falls down. I'm shocked to discover that I'm naked to my waist. Where am I, and what happened last night?

Struggling to remember, I look around. The walls are painted a soft dove gray. The lamps on the reclaimed wood bedside tables are gray with cream shades. A large mother of pearl chandelier hangs from the ceiling.

Strands of memory slowly return. I took off my shirt here last night. Something about it being wet? I threw it to a corner... Ah. There it is, exactly where I remember tossing it, crumpled into a heap next to the window seat. My bra lies next to it.

I dress, wrinkling my nose at the stale smell of beer on my shirt. Slowly, I recollect more. Dr. West and Dr. Long were at the Merry Cockatoo last night. I remember them saying something about roofies. They'd brought me here to sleep it off.

A flush creeps up my cheeks. I'd thrown myself at them. I told them I didn't want to sleep alone and I'd practically rubbed my breasts in their faces.

Yikes. What must they think of me? I bury my face in my hands and shudder in horror. Way to go, Mia.

There's a knock at the door. I look up to see Benjamin Long and Landon West standing in the doorway. They're both dressed casually, in jeans and t-shirts. Thankfully, the t-shirts are free of offensive and dorky slogans. Not that these men would ever need stupid pick-up lines. Women must throw themselves at them all the time.

"You're up," Ben says. "How are you feeling?"

I clutch at the sheet, bringing it up to my chin. "How long have you been standing there?"

Landon's lips twitch. "Don't worry, Mia," he drawls. "We saw plenty last night."

Ben shoots him a quelling look. "You were roofied," he says, confirming my suspicions. "You wouldn't tell us your address, so we brought you here to sleep it off."

"Here? Where exactly am I?"

"My house."

"What happened last night?" My voice comes out in a whisper. "Did we..." I trail off, unable to continue. My face feels like it's on fire. "Did I?"

"Ask us if we wanted you?" Landon's eyes glitter with some unnamed emotion. "Yes, you did."

Ben looks irritated. "Nothing happened, Ms. Gardner," he assures me. "Obviously."

To my horror, my eyes fill with tears. "Obviously?" I choke out before I can stop myself from blurting out those words. "Obviously nothing happened because I'm so boring?" I blink frantically, trying to stop the crying before they notice. "I get it, okay. Guys are bored by me. I'm not Cassie." I hiccup. "And you don't have to be so formal. You can call me Mia."

"What are you talking about?" Ben demands. "You think nothing happened because you're boring? Mia, you were inebriated and drugged. What kind of assholes would we be if we took advantage?"

He called me Mia. I like the way my name sounds on Dr. Long's lips. There's a caress in his tone as he says my name.

And his dick is hard. I can see the outline of his cock through his jeans. My eyes fly to Landon's crotch, and he's turned on too.

Both of them. Because of me.

"Why were you drinking last night?" Landon's voice breaks the momentary silence that's fallen over the room. "Five pints? What on earth were you thinking? You were lucky we were there."

Again, I feel myself flush. Normally, I'd stammer something and run away, but I'm feeling rebellious. "If you insist on knowing," I retort, "I was looking to get laid, okay? That's why I was drinking. I thought that if I was relaxed, that maybe I'd be able to orgasm."

Furiously, I blink back tears from my eyes. God, I sound pathetic and needy and desperate.

"You want to orgasm?" Landon asks me, his voice low and strained. "You think some random dickhead from a bar is going to make you come?"

I glare at him, stung. "Hey, it might not be much of a plan, but it's what I have, okay? It's not like there's a lineup of men offering to date me."

Ben steps into the room and I swallow. All of a sudden, I notice how big he is. Tall, wide shoulders, broad chest. "If you want to orgasm, Mia," he says, his eyes gleaming with heat, "you just have to ask."

"Wait, what?"

"You asked us last night if we wanted you," Landon mutters. "I think the answer is obvious."

I've seen dicks before, but judging from the bulges in their pants, these cocks are in a different league altogether. These are Hall Of Fame Cocks. Trophy Cocks. Cocks of Steel.

And I want them. Being a good girl has got me nowhere. A failed relationship with a cheating ex, who was never interested in what I wanted in bed, and managed to make me feel like shit every time we made love.

Forget Dennis. I want Dr. Long and Dr. West to make me climax.

I drop the sheet, exposing my naked breasts to their gazes. "Yes," I whisper, "please make me come."

The instant I utter those words, it's as if a dam bursts. The two of them stalk toward me, desire etched on their faces. I'm vaguely conscious that I'm a mess; my makeup has smeared on Dr. Long's thousand thread count Egyptian cotton pillow-case, my hair hangs in tangled heaps around my shoulders, and my breath probably reeks of alcohol and desperation.

They don't seem to care. "Get up," Ben orders, his voice steely. "You're going to obey if you want to come, Mia."

I give them a shocked look, and Landon gives me an amused smile. "Remember what you asked for?" he says. "You want to be taken, don't you, Mia? You don't want us to be gentle."

I bite my lip and wordlessly get to my feet. I stand there, naked to my waist, wearing nothing other than a pair of cream lace panties and last night's yellow skirt.

Their eyes rake over me, filling me with burning desire. A hot rush of wetness fills my pussy from the way they're looking at me as if I'm a tasty treat for them to consume, to devour.

"Very nice," Landon purrs. "Are you wearing panties under your skirt, Mia?"

Wordlessly, I nod. I can barely meet their gazes. I'm embarrassed by my arousal. Surely I can't be soaking wet already? All they've done so far is order me to my feet.

"What was that, Mia?" Ben asks silkily. "I didn't hear you."

"Yes, I'm wearing panties."

"Not for long." Landon sits down on the window seat and folds his tattoo-covered arms. His biceps bulge and I stare at the inked dragon on his right forearm, fascinated by the elaborate design. "Take them off and hand them to me, Mia."

Oh God. I can't believe I'm doing this in full sight of the window. We're on the second floor, but if someone's on the street looking up, they can probably see the silhouette of my naked body.

"I'm not a patient man, Mia. If you don't take those panties off in the next ten seconds, I'm tearing them off you myself."

I think I might actually combust. I might drown from the pool of wetness that gushes between my legs at his firm tone. I slide my underwear off quickly. It's tempting to let Landon tear them off me, but I can't go home naked under my skirt. That's just too slutty, and I'm a good girl.

A good girl who's almost naked in front of two men. Okay, I might be a little wilder than I'm giving myself credit for.

Ben holds his hand out for my panties. Blushing, I had them to him, and watch as he sniffs them deeply.

"Smells like pussy?" I snark, unable to help myself.

His eyes twinkle. "I love the smell of panties in the morning," he quips. "Smells like victory." His smile fades. "Walk over to the window," he orders. "Lean over Landon. Put your hands on the seat, on either side of him."

"What?" My heart jumps in shock. "I can't. What if someone sees me?"

Ben tilts his head to one side and waits.

"It's too embarrassing," I wail.

He doesn't reply.

Damn it. The message is clear. If I obey, they'll make me come.

And I really want to come.

Ah well. So what if someone sees me? After all, I'm single. Unlike Dennis *Limp Dick* Burrows, I'm not a cheater.

With shaking legs, I walk over to where Landon's sitting. As Ben instructs, I bend at my waist and place my hands on either side of Landon's legs. My face is inches from Landon's, and my breasts hang down, my nipples almost grazing his thighs. My ass sticks up lewdly in the air.

"Very good, Mia," Benjamin says approvingly. He moves behind me, and his palm caresses my butt before spanking me hard.

"Hey," I protest, though I don't move away. I don't want to. Landon's fingers move to my nipples, and he pinches them gently. Pleasure fills me, radiates from my nipples and warms the rest of my body.

"Stop overthinking this," Landon says. "Just let yourself feel."

Ben's palms run over my butt cheeks, stroking me. His fingers dip lower, teasing at my crease. I groan and thrust my ass toward him, spreading my legs wider so he has easier access to my pussy. A little voice in the back of my mind warns me that I'm being a slut, but just then, Ben's finger circles my clitoris, and I push that voice away. *Not now, self-loathing conscience. We'll talk later.*

I had to draw Dennis a map to my clitoris. Ben has no trouble finding the perfect spot to touch me. Perhaps he has pussy GPS.

Landon's arms close over mine, and he repositions me with my palms flat on the window behind him. In this position, his mouth is inches from my breasts, and he takes full advantage, nibbling at my rosy tips.

My heart races in my chest. I just stand there, legs open, my tits thrust into Landon's mouth, sighing with pleasure. This feels so good. My knees threaten to buckle under the sheer heat of their onslaught.

"So you want both of us at once, Mia?" Benjamin's thumb circles my anus. "You want a cock in your pussy and one in your ass?" His finger pushes into my tight opening, and his tongue swipes a long, leisurely path up my cleft before pressing down on my clitoris. I exhale hard as my entire body tightens from the unexpected heat.

"Answer him." Landon's voice is rough.

"Yes," I breathe. What's the point in pretending? I've already told them my darkest fantasies, and they don't appear to be disgusted by them. When I was hypnotized, I told them I wanted both of them, and here they are, touching me, stroking me, spanking me.

Benjamin's thumb feels so large in my ass. A little weird and a lot naughty, but mostly good. While he's getting me accustomed to the unexpected intrusion, his fingers push into my pussy. "You're so fucking tight," he grinds out.

"When I fill you with my cock, you're not going to be able to walk straight for a week."

Oh my fucking God. Benjamin Long is a secret dirty talker. Underneath the expensive suits and the calm facade, he's got a smutty, smutty mouth.

And I love it.

"I'm going to take you while you wrap your sweet little lips around Landon's dick," he promises. His thumb wriggles deeper, almost to the first knuckle. It's uncomfortable, and it's thrilling, and I never want him to stop.

Landon pushes my breasts together and lowers his mouth to them. He bites and teases one bud after another. When I'm suitably distracted, Benjamin pushes his thumb deeper into me, burying the full length of his finger in my ass.

"So tight," he groans. "Like a fucking vise, Mia. I'm going to enjoy taking you here..." He half-pulls his thumb out and pushes it back in again, and I rock forward, my breasts grinding into Landon's face.

He doesn't appear to mind. His mouth clamps down harder over my nipples, his big hands kneading my globes. Benjamin's fingers strum over my clitoris, tracing increasingly tighter circles. My muscles tighten.

Usually, this is the point when I tense up, wondering if I'm going to finally have an orgasm that isn't caused by my own fingers. And because I'm focusing on whether it's going to happen or not, the moment slips away.

But things are different this time. This time, there's two of them.

As Benjamin's fingers pump in and out of my pussy, Landon's teeth nip at my breasts. Pleasure pummels me from all directions.

Then Benjamin spanks my ass hard, and I explode with

a shriek. The muscles in my pussy quiver and grab onto his fingers, and I slump against Landon's hard chest.

Landon smiles smugly. "Was that an orgasm?" he asks, his eyes dancing with amusement. "I couldn't tell."

"Ass." I break out into a wide smile. I can't believe it. I just came. Not with Mr. Rabbit, not with my fingers. A man made me come. Well, two men. Though Ben was responsible for the actual deed, Landon certainly played a key role.

Benjamin grins as he takes a seat next to Landon. "Mia," he asks me, "would you like some breakfast?"

10

LANDON

Well, well. Mia might be a good girl, but she has a wild side.

Pulling Mia down on my lap, I savor the feel of her round ass grinding against my dick. I'm rock hard and aching for release, and I'm more than a little jealous that Ben got to taste her.

Belatedly, my conscience makes an appearance. Mia got roofied last night. She's woken up in Ben's guest bedroom, and she's just come. She's not thinking straight.

Don't get me wrong—I want her. I want to plunge my cock into her tight little pussy and take her, but it's important for her to want the same thing. Mia seems pretty sheltered, and though she dreams about two men taking her, she might not want to act on her fantasies.

"Mia." I wrap my arms around her waist and breathe in the aroma of her hair. She smells like jasmine and roses, and for a second, my resolve wobbles.

"Landon." Her voice comes out as a sigh. She turns around, squirming on my lap, and addresses the two of us.

"Thank you so much." A blush rises over her lovely cheeks. "I should return the favor."

Sometimes, I wish I could think with my dick. The thought of being buried in her soft channel is so tempting. "As much as I'd like that," I tell her seriously, "I don't want you to feel pressured into anything."

She opens her mouth to say something, and I hold up my hand to forestall her. "Take some time to think about it, and if you still want both of us, join us for dinner tonight."

Ben slants a look in my direction. "Part of me wants to call Landon a cock-blocker," he grumbles to Mia. "But he's right."

I can't read the expression on Mia's face. "What time is dinner?" she asks. "And can I bring dessert?"

"Seven," I reply at once. "And Mia, you'll be dessert."

Mia leaves right after breakfast, and as much as I want to talk to Ben about what happened, I don't have time to linger either; I have to go to work. Neither Benjamin nor I particularly enjoy working over the weekend, but it's an unavoidable part of our business. Our clients lead busy lives, and often, the only available time they have to meet us is over the weekend. Over the years, we've honed our schedules so that each of us is only working one Saturday a month.

It's a lovely late summer morning as I walk to my house to take a quick shower before heading to the office. There's almost no one on the tree-lined streets, and in the quiet, I can hear the sound of birds chirping. On mornings like these, I don't miss Manhattan at all.

Sophia's in the kitchen making herself some toast when I walk in. "Where were you last night?" she asks me, then shakes her head. "Never mind, don't tell me. I don't want to hear about my big brother's sex life. Too awkward."

"As if I'm going to tell you anything." I snag a piece of

buttered toast off her plate, ignoring her indignant look. "I checked out your bar last night."

"And?" My baby sister gives me a hopeful look. "Was it okay?"

Fuck no. It wasn't okay at all. Some assholes roofied Mia and Cassie's drinks. I don't want Sophia anywhere near that place.

Except Sophia isn't a child anymore. The more protective I am, the more she's going to rebel. In a year, she'll be eighteen, and she won't have to listen to my advice anymore. I can't bark orders at Sophia and expect her to obey.

"A couple of women got roofied there last night," I tell her. "Once Nina Templeton found out, she threw the assholes that did it out of the bar, but I still worry about you, Soph. It makes me nervous that you'll be hanging out in such an environment."

She butters her toast. "I'm a minor," she replies. "I won't be in the bar at all."

"I know." I've been her big brother all my life, but I can't stop her from growing up. "Promise me you won't drink there."

A wide smile breaks out on her face. "I promise," she replies readily. "Landon, trust me. I want to be a chef. Drinking is the last thing on my mind."

"In that case, apply away, kiddo." I glance at my watch and get to my feet. "I need to head to work, and I'm not going to be home tonight again. No wild parties, okay?"

Her eyes narrow speculatively. "Two nights in a row? Who is your mystery woman?"

I shake my head at her. I don't even know why Sophia bothers asking. She knows I don't discuss my personal life with anyone.

I arrive at work an hour earlier than my first appointment. To my surprise, Amy's there, and worse, she's not in the reception area; she's in my office rummaging through something in my filing cabinet.

She jumps when I walk in. "Hello Landon," she stammers. "I didn't expect to see you this early."

I frown. It's Saturday; our receptionist doesn't work weekends. I have no idea what she's doing here. "Why are you here?" I ask bluntly. "And what do you need in my office?"

Her eyes drop to the floor. "I wasn't sure if I'd readied Mr. Wallace's paperwork for your appointment this morning," she replies. "I don't live very far away, so I thought I'd come in and check."

Yeah right. Amy's going to double-check her work when pigs fly. I give her a skeptical look. "That's why you're here?"

She clears her throat. "There's another reason," she admits. "I was hoping to talk to you when Dr. Long wasn't around."

I don't have time for Amy. Jason Wallace will be here soon enough, and I need to reread the notes on his case and think about his treatment plan. "I'm a little busy this morning, Amy," I say bluntly. "Can we keep this quick?"

She meets my gaze boldly. "I was wondering if you wanted to go out sometime. You know, like a date?"

Damn it. I should have guessed that this is what this is about. Amy's been hinting that she'd like to go out with me ever since she started working for us. Unfortunately, even if she wasn't an employee, I'm not interested. There's a mean and judgmental streak in Amy, and I can't abide people like that.

Still, I try and let her down easily. "I'm sorry, Amy. You're an employee. I can't date you—that violates my professional ethics."

"Really?" Her eyebrows rise. "You left the Merry Cock-atoo with Mia Gardner last night. She's a patient, isn't she?" An ugly expression flits across her face. "I'm sure the College of Psychotherapists would be very interested in knowing you're sleeping with a patient."

"Ms. Gardner isn't a patient." I don't know why I'm even explaining myself to our receptionist. "She decided against using our services after an initial consultation."

My blood boils. I respond very poorly to threats, and I cannot believe that Amy Cooke is trying to blackmail me. Dr. Bollington is the local Head of the College, and I know he'd love an opportunity to embroil us in a witch-hunt investigation.

We tried to give Amy a second chance, but she doesn't seem to want to take it. I reach a quick decision. We cannot have someone work at our practice that we do not trust. Given the nature of what we do, confidentiality is an abso-lute must. "You're fired," I say bluntly. "Pack up your belong-ings and leave."

"What?" Her voice is thin with shock.

"You heard me."

I watch the news sink in, then Amy's face contorts with rage. "This is because of that bitch, isn't it?" she sneers. "Mia fucking Gardner. Well, you'll soon tire of her. She won't give you what you need. She can't even get her fiancé to keep it in his pants. As if she's going to keep your interest."

"Pack your stuff," I repeat, my voice dangerous. *How dare this bitch talk about Mia.* "And get out. Now."

11

MIA

I should be mortified that I'm doing the walk of shame, but I feel like dancing through the streets as I walk home. *I had an orgasm,* I want to yell out loud. Landon West pinched my nipples, and Benjamin Long licked my pussy and thrust his fingers into me, and I actually came.

I'm so thrilled I don't even have time to dwell on the fact that someone roofied Cassie and me last night. Ben told me over breakfast that Kelli was at home last night when they dropped Cassie off. Thank heavens. Kelli's a nurse. She would have known what to do.

My cheeks warm as I remember propositioning them last night. Memory is a funny thing. I don't remember them showing up at the bar, and I don't remember the drive back, but I do remember them rejecting me last night.

And I have a date with them tonight. Both of them. Lust floods my body, and I shiver. Ben had a finger in my ass this morning. Will it be his cock tonight? I've never had anal sex before. Oh, who am I kidding? I've never had much of anything other than straight-up missionary. I'm pretty sure I can count on one hand how many times Dennis went down on me.

I shower quickly and manage to open my boutique just in time. I don't even have a moment to pop in and check on Cassie. I do have time to text her though, and she replies right away, which is a relief. *She's fine.*

It's usually quite empty in the mornings, and I don't expect to be very busy. To my surprise, there's a steady stream of shoppers all morning. All locals, all there to ask about last night. If there's one thing New Summit runs on, it's gossip.

Nina's the first visitor. "Oh my God, Mia," she exclaims. "I can't believe those guys last night. Thank goodness Dr. West and Dr. Long were around to take Cassie and you home. I threw those assholes out, and I called the cops. I'm so sorry."

"It's not your fault," I reassure her. "You're not responsible for what those guys did. Do you know who they are? I didn't recognize them. Are they from New Summit?"

She shakes her head. "I took photos of their drivers' licenses before throwing them out," she replies. "I think they're from Jersey."

"Have you looked in on Cassie?"

She nods. "Yeah, she's nursing quite a hangover. She gulped down all of her roofied wine. You, on the other hand, were so drunk you spilled half of it down your shirt."

"Don't remind me," I groan. "I'm trying to forget how wasted I was."

She laughs. "It's not a bad thing for you to cut loose once in a while," she says. "I just need to keep a closer eye on your drinks." Her eyes scan the room, and her expression brightens. "God, that's a pretty dress."

She moves over and pulls out a red wrap dress. "Try it

on," I encourage. "You can take advantage of the friends-and-family discount."

"Really? How large is this discount?"

"For you, twenty-five percent."

Taking advantage of New Summit's relentless desire for gossip, I sell three dresses, four sweaters, and two skirts before eleven. I've just closed the register on the last transaction when Cassie pushes open the door. "Kill me," she groans. "Everyone in New Summit must have been at my coffee shop this morning."

"The ones that weren't here," I quip. "Did you save me a carrot muffin?"

"Of course" She hands me the treat and a cup of coffee, and I sigh in pleasure as I sink onto my loveseat and kick off my pumps.

"How are you feeling?" I ask her.

"I feel like I've been pounded with a baseball bat," she says with a grimace. "Kelli tells me that's normal. You?"

I can't stop the grin that's breaking out on my face. "I feel great."

"Whoa there, Nellie." She takes a large gulp of her coffee and gives me a pointed look. "You're suspiciously cheerful. I thought you'd be blaming yourself for getting roofied, but no, you look happy. What's going on?"

"Umm, why would I blame myself for getting roofied?" I ask through a mouthful of carrot muffin.

She rolls her eyes. "Good girls don't get drunk." She mimics my voice with startling accuracy. "That's why."

"Oh." I wince at how prissy that makes me sound. "Well, I am happy." I glance around the shop to make sure it's empty, then I lean toward Cassie. "Remember my sex problem? Solved."

She looks blank for a second, then understanding dawns

on her face. "You hooked up?" she yelps. "Who with?" Then she puts two and two together. "Oh my God, you hooked up with one of the sexy psychotherapists? Which one?"

I feel the blush creep up my cheeks. "Both of them," I whisper.

Cassie's mouth drops open. "What? At the same time?" She fans herself dramatically. "My little girl's growing up and jumping on the threesome train. I'm so proud."

"Will you stop that?" I hiss at her. "It's not a big deal."

She gapes at me. "Not a big deal?" she asks. "What are you talking about? It's a huge deal. Normally, you never put a toe out of place, and last night you had a threesome?" She pauses for a second. "Wait a second, those jerks didn't take advantage of you, did they?"

"No, of course not," I assure her. "Nothing happened last night. It was this morning. And we didn't go all the way. Their pants stayed on. On the other hand, my panties," I smirk proudly, "did not."

"Who are you, and what have you done with my best friend?" Cassie demands.

"I know, right?" I chew on my muffin. "I'm seeing them again tonight."

"Bow chika wow wow," she sing-songs cheerfully. Cassie's awesome. Not a word of judgment, not a sliver of disapproval. "I'm so glad for you, Mia. After a year of Dennis, you deserve something good in your life."

Thinking of Dennis makes me wince. I haven't thought of him at all this week. At some point, I'm going to have to talk to him and tell him to stop calling or texting me. Not yet though.

"Help me find a dress to wear tonight, Cass?"

She laughs. "Mia, you run a boutique. You have amazing taste. You don't need my help."

"Yes, I do," I insist. "I'm a nervous wreck about this date. These guys are way out of my league."

"No, they're not," she replies, getting to her feet. "You're awesome, and you're going to show them that tonight. Let's find you something to wear."

We find a dress. Cassie gets back to her coffee shop, and I help the steady stream of shoppers find what they need. Before I know it, it's six in the evening. Time to get ready for my date.

I'm flipping the sign on the front door to *'Closed'*, preparing to leave, when Dennis walks in, looking worried. "I just heard about last night, Mia," he says, enveloping me in a hug. "Are you okay?"

I stiffen in his embrace and wrench myself free of his grasp. "I'm fine," I tell him. "Thanks for checking."

"You're still mad at me," he says unhappily. "Mia, I'm sorry, I really am. It was just that..." His voice trails off.

"It was just that what?" I ask, narrowing my eyes. I'd love to know what his excuse is.

"Well," he says after a brief hesitation, "I mean, come on, Mia. Men have needs."

"And women don't?" My voice rises in annoyance. A week ago, I'd have told myself that nice girls don't scream, but I'm too irritated with my stupid, sniveling ex-fiancé right now. "I've heard all about your needs, Dennis. What about mine? Did you ever think about that?"

He pats my back in a patronizing gesture that has me gritting my teeth. "You're upset," he soothes. "That's understandable." He clears his throat. "Mia, I didn't come here to fight with you. I came to ask you to get back together with me."

"Why?" The clock on the wall behind his head is showing that it's a quarter after six. I want to shower before my date, and it'll take me ten minutes to walk to Ben's house. I don't have time for Dennis right now. "I'm not interested in getting back together," I tell him bluntly. "Go find Tiffany Slater."

"There's someone else, isn't there?" A look of suspicion washes over his face. "I heard that those two shrinks gave you a ride home last night. Is it one of them?"

I wish I could just blurt out to Dennis what I did to Cassie. I wish I could confess that I'm going to hook up with both of them, but I'm not brave enough to do that. It's one thing to tell my best friend. It's another thing entirely to admit the truth to Dennis or anyone else. All day, I've been the center of attention because of last night's attempted roofie, and I've hated every minute of it. I don't like living in the spotlight.

"That's none of your business," I snap, my patience wearing thin. "You cheated on me two hours after you asked me to marry you. We're not a couple anymore. I don't answer to you." I push him toward the door. "Stop calling me. My phone keeps ringing at work, and it's very annoying."

"Mia," he splutters. "You're being hasty."

Oh no, I'm not. "Goodbye, Dennis." I shut the door behind him and lock it, feeling a sense of satisfaction as I do so. Cassie's right. Dennis was never into me. I was just someone who would make a good wife. Our relationship was all about his needs.

I shower quickly and slip on the green cotton dress with white piping that Cassie and I chose earlier. It's cute, and it brings out the color in my eyes, but it's not a 'fuck-me-now' dress. As much as I wish I had the nerve to be able to wear one of those, I don't. I'm not the femme fatale type; I'm the girl next door. This dress plays to my strengths.

Butterflies dance in my stomach as I head out.
I'm going to have a threesome tonight.
Me, Mia Gardner.
Part of me is in shock at my daring.
This feels momentous.

I've never yet met someone who didn't like lasagna, so that's what I cook. To go with it, I make a simple tossed salad. Mesclun lettuce, locally grown cherry tomatoes, Kalamata olives, and buffalo mozzarella, dressed simply with extra-virgin olive oil and balsamic vinegar.

It takes me a couple of hours to put everything together. As I fry the ground beef before layering it with the pasta, I try and wonder when I last made this much effort for a woman. I never cooked for Becky; we ate at fancy restaurants in Manhattan. Every time I contemplated making a meal for her, I decided the mess in the kitchen just wasn't worth it.

I'm not sure what's different now. Maybe it's because my kitchen in New Summit is much larger than the one in my SoHo condo. Maybe it's easier to cook when sunlight streams in through the patio doors that form the back wall of the space. Maybe it's because I can hear the birds chirp as I dice tomatoes for a marinara sauce.

Or maybe it's the woman I'm cooking for.

Landon and I have shared women before. Not recently,

and never seriously. As I cook, I find myself wondering how things would work if we were actually in a relationship with Mia. New Summit is a gossipy small town. Many of the long-time residents are scandalized by our unconventional therapy techniques. Despite the miracles they perform, surrogates are widely considered only a step above sex workers. Dr. Bollington, the local Head of the College, has openly called for us to shut down our practice.

Despite his opposition, we're busier than we expected to be. People approach us discreetly, looking for help with their sexual problems. Landon and I have saved more marriages and relationships than we can count. It's that sense of satisfaction that keeps us going. God knows neither of us needs the money from our practice—we each earn an obscene amount of money from the self-help books we've co-authored.

A few minutes before seven, there's a knock on the patio doors, and Landon walks in, holding a bottle of red wine. Shortly after that, Mia shows up, and Landon lets her in while I pull the bread out of the oven and arrange it on a platter.

"Wow, it smells great in here."

I stop what I'm doing and take her in. Her green dress fits her perfectly, and she looks fresh-faced and radiantly beautiful.

She does not look like the kind of girl that takes part in a threesome. Looks can sometimes be deceiving.

"You look like a piece of candy," I tell her with a grin.

She laughs. "I've never been called that before." She eyes the food with wonder. "You cooked. I wouldn't have pegged either of you as the cooking type."

"I'm full of surprises."

Landon rolls his eyes. "Mia, would you like something to drink? Wine, beer or champagne?"

"Wine please," she replies. "After last night, I might stay away from beer for a week or two."

The three of us take our seats. I've taken the time to set the table, another thing I never did with Becky. Tea lights flicker in shallow glass containers and the large bouquet of hydrangeas adds some color to my slate gray appliances. "I thought we'd eat here," I say, gesturing to the open patio doors. "It's a nice evening. Might as well take advantage."

Mia takes her seat and looks around. "This is lovely," she says. "You've done a great job with the renovation."

I raise my eyebrow, as does Landon. "How do you know I've been renovating?" I ask her.

She laughs. "It's New Summit," she replies. "Everyone knows everything. This house used to be in horrible shape. You're quite a hero in town because you fixed it up."

"That's good to know," I say dryly. "Landon and I don't feel popular."

Her lips twist into a rueful grimace. "Dr. Bollington giving you grief?" she guesses astutely. "Ignore him. He's my landlord. When he's not complaining about Cassie, he's bitching about Nina and the Merry Cockatoo. Honestly, if there was nothing to grumble about, I don't know what he'd do with his time."

"He's not busy with his practice?" Landon interjects.

She shakes her head. "Not really," she says, lifting her shoulders in a shrug. "He's always so judgmental that I wouldn't go to him for help. Would you?"

That explains a lot of Bollington's opposition to us. The man's clearly threatened.

The conversation flows easily between us. We talk about the books we've read lately, and the movies we've seen.

Eventually, the topic returns to our work. "Do you get turned on?" Mia asks, leaning forward, her cheeks pink. "When women are voicing their fantasies in your office?"

"Not before you," Landon replies.

Time for me to level up. "I have a confession to make," I tell her. "We don't generally suggest surrogates until we've tried other avenues, and we don't actually watch the sex happen. But I was really attracted to you, and I wanted to see you again. If you became a patient, that could have never happened, so I might have exaggerated things a little."

"You scared me away!" She sounds indignant, but her eyes sparkle with merriment. "That's terrible."

I wince. "Yeah. Sorry about that."

She chuckles. "That's okay, Ben. I was just messing with you. Honestly, even if you hadn't suggested surrogates, I wouldn't have come back."

"Why?" Landon leans forward, his expression intent. "Why wouldn't you have come back?"

"I was too attracted to you," she whispers. "I would have spent every session fantasizing about the two of you."

13

MIA

The way they look at me, it's as if they want to devour me.

Landon gets to his feet. He takes the wine glass from my suddenly nerveless fingers. "It's time," he says in a low voice, "to live the fantasy. Are you ready, Mia? Do you want this?"

"Yes."

"In that case, let's move this to the bedroom," Ben says smoothly. Good idea. The doors to the patio are open, and I'm pretty sure they're going to make me scream with pleasure tonight.

I'm not going to lie. I'm a little nervous. I don't have a lot of experience, and they clearly do. I don't want to bore them with my fumbling attempts at being alluring.

Before I can second-guess myself, Landon scoops me into his arms, making me squeal in surprise. "You're frowning, Mia," he accuses me. "Do you want to change your mind?"

I shake my head. No. I definitely don't want to change my mind.

"Then stop stressing." He pushes open the bedroom door with his leg and tosses me on the bed. Ben is only a half-step behind.

I scoot back against the headboard, my heart beating faster. If I were more confident, I might lay back on the bed and show off my body, but I'm the girl that needed to be hypnotized so I could blurt out what turns me on. Coming here has taken all the courage I have.

Ben and Landon close on the bed, and I breathe faster. They're so unbelievably hot.

Ben's eyes rake my body. My dress has ridden up around my legs, and plenty of bare skin is on display. "You look good enough to eat," he says.

"Now there's an idea." Landon rolls up his shirtsleeves before prowling toward me. "I've been waiting to taste you all day," he growls.

He leans down and grabs my ankles, drawing me back to the edge of the bed. He slides me down until my ass is almost hanging off, and my green dress ends up above my hips. I get a thrill as Landon kneels down on the floor.

Oral sex is a rare treat in my world. Dennis was missionary all the way.

"Such a sweet pussy," he breathes, yanking my panties out of the way. He props my calves over his shoulders and cups my buttocks in his large hands before lowering his head between my legs.

I don't mean to, but I tense. Hey, I've had a year of bad sex, and until this morning, no orgasms. Ben was great this morning, and I have no reason to believe it won't be great with Landon.

"You're so tense, Mia." Instead of diving right in, Landon turns his head and presses a kiss to my inner thigh. I shiver as his stubble tickles my sensitive skin.

Ben comes to my side. I'm at the perfect height to see the bulge under his zipper. "Give me your hand." He presses my fingers against the front of his pants, and I trace the hard ridge of his cock through the fabric. It's massive and straining to break free.

"Oh wow." My nipples harden.

A smile creases Ben's face. "You told us you wanted to be pushed against a wall, Mia," he says. "Remember? You wanted us to pull your hands above your head and hold them in place."

I flush as he continues. "You want us to be forceful, Mia? You want to be taken?"

This is it. I can either embrace my fantasies, or I can do what I've done my entire life. Hidden from my needs, pretending I don't crave this. I could go back to another year of Dennis *Limp Dick* Burrows.

"Take me." I bite my lower lip. I feel so wanton right now. I can barely meet Ben's eyes.

His expression isn't judgmental or condemning. No, he looks like Christmas came early. And *I* put that expression on his face.

His hand strokes my face and cups my jaw. Then his expression becomes steelier. "You're going to suck me off while Landon pleasures you," he commands. "I've been waiting all day to have this mouth on me, and you're going to be a good girl and give me what I want." He sets a finger at my mouth, and I open, sucking the digit in and swirling my tongue around it.

Meanwhile, Landon lays his mouth over my pussy, and my entire body clenches at his touch. His tongue presses in my cleft. It's the lightest stroke, the perfect amount of pressure. I lift my hips off the bed, searching for more.

"You smell delicious," he rasps. His tongue glides over my heated flesh, awakening every cell in my body.

"Mia," Ben chastises. "Focus. You have a cock to suck." His cock is out now, and he's pulling on it gently with one hand. His other cups my breast, squeezing a little. The casual claiming makes me gasp, and I grind my hips into Landon's mouth.

"Ask him, Mia." Landon sits back on his haunches and surveys me. "Ask him for permission to suck his cock. Tell him you want to take him down your throat."

I'm so turned on that I can't breathe.

"Please can I," I start to say, but Landon's tongue steals the rest of my sentence. Wet and relentless, it swoops right over my clit. My hips jerk and my breath comes faster. Oh God.

It's like the universe is watching out for me. Rewarding me for a lifetime of horrible sex.

Thank you, universe.

Landon's finger finds my entrance and slips inside. "Oh God," I moan again.

His lips twist into a smug grin. "You can call me Landon," he quips, looking like a cat with cream. His tongue flicks against my clit while his index finger hooks inside, searching for my G-spot. The sensation makes my pussy clench.

Above me, Ben chuckles. "Responsive little thing, isn't she?"

Crap. I'm supposed to be sucking Ben off. I reach for his cock, my lips parted open, my body prickling with anticipation. His cock is hard and velvety smooth, and my fingers close around the base, stroking his shaft. He kneels on the bed, positioning himself so that he's above me. "Open," he orders.

I take the head in my mouth, feeling triumphant when a groan escapes his lips. I lick his length, before taking him as deep as I can, swallowing around his cock.

Just then, Landon moves his finger out of my pussy and sets it to the rim of my bottom hole. He teases my anus, circling the tightly puckered hole before he slides the tip in.

I almost jump off the bed. Ben's lips quirk at my response. Reaching across me, he cups my breast, his thumb teasing the nipple and his strong forearm holding me down on the bed. "Stay where you are," he says calmly.

Another shudder of arousal runs through me, and my bottom clenches around Landon's invading digit.

"One finger and you're jumping off the bed," Landon says to me, his tone amused. "But this is just the beginning, Mia. You're going to learn to take both of us, aren't you?"

"Answer him." Ben grips my breast hard.

"Yes," I pant through a mouthful of cock. I'll say anything as long as they keep touching me.

Satisfied, Landon bows his head and returns to flicking his tongue at my pulsing clitoris. My legs tremble. Ben thrusts into my mouth, pinching my nipple at the same time with a wicked smile on his face.

It's too much. Too much is happening at once.

I pull free of Ben's cock, not trusting myself to keep my mouth slack in the throes of my climax. That's the last coherent thought I have. My body arcs off the bed, my head falls back, and I shatter.

When I catch my breath, both men loom over me. "It's our turn now," Landon says with a smirk.

So far, I'm at two orgasms—one this morning, and one just now. I'm more than ready to even up the score. "Seems fair to me."

"Dress off," Ben orders. I'm still shaky, my head fuzzy

from my orgasm, so Ben helps me, whipping it over my head.

Landon moves behind me to unhook my bra and pulls it down my arms. I lean back into him, my bare back meeting his bare chest. I don't remember him getting naked, but then again, I've been a little distracted. Really good orgasms will do that to a girl.

Once the bra is off, I half-turn to ogle at him. Lean and cut, his body is positively mouthwatering, and I'm mesmerized by the play of muscles of his chest and abs.

"I seem to recall," he says, "that your fantasies included being tied up." The corners of his eyes crinkle as he smiles. "Arms behind your back."

I comply, and Landon positions my hands above my head, tying them loosely with my own bra. "If you get nervous," he mutters, "a good tug and they'll come undone."

I appreciate the consideration. He positions me so I'm lying back on the bed. Ben moves into the space between my legs, also naked, while Landon kneels on the mattress, his cock inches from my face. His penis is large and a little intimidating. I crane my neck forward and lick the tip, looking up at him for approval.

"Fuck, Mia," he groans. "You're the most beautiful thing I've ever seen." He pushes further into my mouth. I warm up, bobbing my head, letting him stretch my jaw wide and giving him lots of tongue. I want to see him lose control.

Ben growls. "Fuck Mia," he murmurs. "Now there's a great idea." He grips my thighs with his big hands and spreads me wide open. Rolling a condom on, he positions the head of his cock at my pussy.

I almost sob. I've been waiting for this moment all evening. "You're going to suck Landon's cock while I fuck you, Mia," Ben orders. "Open your mouth wide, Mia. Show him how much you want him."

I gasp around Landon's cock as Ben pushes into my pussy with one hard thrust. Landon holds me in place, his fingers wrapping around my hair. "It's quite hard to maintain a rhythm when Ben's fucking you," he says, "but you're going to try, Mia. Isn't that right?"

Holy smokes. I told them I wanted a forceful and dominant man, and my God, did they deliver. Every smoothly voiced order causes a fresh burst of heat to rush to my pussy. Every dirty command out of their mouths causes me to shiver, consumed by lust.

"You are so fucking tight, Mia," Ben says, his teeth clenched. "I'm going to come in this sweet little pussy." His fingers dig into my thighs as he rocks deeper into me.

I moan around Landon's cock as Ben's thrusts increase in intensity. Landon's close too. His grip on my hair tightens. "You're going to swallow, aren't you baby?"

You can bet your life on it.

Ben's fingers move to my clitoris, circling that over sensitized bud again. I whimper, but I don't pull away—I'm greedy like that. Then Landon's cock jerks in my mouth, and I swallow frantically. Ben's fingers increase their pressure while his hard cock rams into my aching pussy. We both come within seconds of each other. Sated, I slump back against the bed.

"Wow," I say softly when the fog in my brain clears. "Thank you."

I thought good sex was a myth. I thought there was something wrong with me because no man had ever made me come, but in the last twelve hours, I've come three times. This might be some kind of world record. Someone should call the Guinness people.

"I'm not sure why you're thanking us," Ben says. "But if you give us about fifteen minutes, we'll do that again."

"Again?"

Landon gives me an amused look. "Why not?" he asks. Then his body moves over mine, and I can't think anymore.

After a second and third round, I'm too drained to move. "I should go," I groan, opening one eye and looking at the time. It's two thirty in the morning. I have never been up this late having sex. That thought makes me smile again.

"Don't," Ben whispers sleepily at my side. "Spend the night."

"Really?" It seems like such an intimate thing to do.

"Really." Landon's arm curls around my waist, holding me against his body. "Please?"

"Okay." *They're just being polite Mia,* I warn myself, though my heart thumps in my chest. Ben and Landon are obviously used to women throwing themselves at them. It wouldn't do to get too attached.

14

MIA

We spend most of Sunday together. Ben makes breakfast, and after we eat, the three of us get in Landon's car and head to the marina, detouring only to get me a fresh set of clothes. "I have a boat docked there," Landon says casually. "Do you sail?"

I roll my eyes. Sailing is a hobby for rich people. Landon and Ben evidently have a lot more money than I do. "No, I don't sail," I say dryly.

Landon winks at me. "I'll teach you, Mia."

I have a great time. After spending the day on the water, we go to a great Thai place for dinner, then to a jazz bar for drinks after. It's ten in the night by the time we get back to New Summit.

"Spend the night," Ben says. "Please?"

"Really?" I give them a teasing look. "Two nights in a row?"

Ben shrugs. "So what? Who's keeping track?" He gives Landon a sidelong look. "Is Sophia expecting you?"

My heart stops. Sophia? Who's Sophia?

My expression must change because Landon chuckles.

"Sophia's my teenage sister," he says. "And no, she's not expecting me."

I'm not prepared for the relief that floods my body. What the hell, Mia? I ask myself. There's two of them. You can't get seriously involved. Play it cool.

On Monday morning, I leave Ben's place later than I expected. I hurry to my apartment and change my clothes quickly, then run to the store so I can be there in time for the delivery guy. These are the days when I'm really glad I don't have a long commute to work.

Unfortunately, the first person that walks through my boutique door is Dennis. "Where were you all of yesterday?" he demands accusingly. "I stopped by at midnight, and you weren't here."

"So?" I give him a bland look.

"You're seeing one of those sex doctors, aren't you?" He gives me a disapproving look. "Do you know that people have sex in their office? They call that therapy, the sick perverts."

"I don't know why you keep coming around here, Dennis," I tell him tiredly. "We're not dating anymore. Find someone else to bother, and leave me alone."

There's a dark look on his face. Dennis isn't used to me standing up to him. My sudden backbone must come as quite a surprise.

15

BENJAMIN

Landon and I get to work earlier than normal on Monday. I completely support Landon's decision to fire Amy; that woman was trouble. But there's no doubt that her absence has created a lot of extra work for us. "We need to find a new receptionist," I mutter as I check the voicemail that's come in over the weekend and prepare to return a dozen phone calls.

Landon, who is tackling the fifty unread emails, all from existing and prospective clients, nods in agreement. "Someone reliable," he says. "Mia grew up here. She might be able to recommend someone."

"Good idea." Amy came to us courtesy of George Bollington. We won't be asking him for help again.

We work in silence for an hour. Once we're caught up, I glance up at Landon. "Speaking of Mia, her shop's not open today, is it?"

Landon shakes his head. "No, why?"

Opening a cabinet at my desk, I pull out a butt plug, new in its packaging. "Because I thought we'd introduce her to this."

Landon grins widely. "I like the way you think," he says. "We don't have clients until two this afternoon, do we?" He pulls his phone out and texts Mia. "Let's see if she can drop by now."

Her response arrives almost immediately. Just one word, but it makes the blood roar in my veins. "Yes."

Mia is wearing a flared red skirt and a black and white striped t-shirt. She looks adorable. "Hey," she greets us with a shy smile. "Landon said you had plans for me."

"You wanted to be taken by both of us at the same time, I believe." I grin wickedly as I hold up the plug. "Your wish is my command."

Her eyes go round.

Landon steps up to her. "Let's get you undressed," he murmurs, his gaze heavy with lust.

Mia bites her lips, and the pulse at her neck speeds up. Her eyes heat with anticipation as Landon's fingers skim over her full breasts before he tugs her shirt over her head. She's wearing a black satin bra underneath, and the color is a stark contrast to her creamy skin.

Landon's fingers skate over her nipples, and they pebble under the bra. He presses her tits together and squeezes hard. Mia gasps and leans closer to him. "Do that again," she whispers, and he squeezes her erect nubs between his thumb and forefinger.

"You like that, you naughty girl?" Watching Mia shudder under Landon's attention, my cock aches with need. I take a deep breath and reach for self-control. This is not about my bone-deep desire to throw Mia across my desk and plunge my dick into her hot pussy. This is about me giving her what she wants, what she needs, but is too embarrassed to ask for.

Landon lifts Mia's skirt up, exposing the round curve of her glorious ass. I inhale sharply as her black satin panties come into view. The briefs hug her curves. A shiver runs across her as her skin is exposed to the air-conditioning in my office.

I can't stand it anymore. I stalk next to them, grabbing the hem of Mia's skirt and tucking it into her waistband. I yank her panties down to her ankles and bend her over my desk. "Spread your legs," I order, my voice tight with arousal.

She's a sight for sore eyes. Her breasts pressed against the wooden surface of my desk, her cleavage spilling out from the bra, her breathing coming in soft pants. I'm never going to look at my office the same way again. I'm going to remember this moment for the rest of my life.

I bend down and kiss a path from her neck down her spine. When I reach the small of her back, I grip her flesh and thrust two fingers into her pussy.

Mia groans and parts her leg wider. She arches her back, trying to push my fingers deeper into her tight channel. "No, no," I chide. "You're always in such a hurry, baby. Slow down and enjoy the moment."

I spank her ass, and the sound of the slap is loud in the quiet room. Thank heavens we fired Amy. I can picture the nosy receptionist with her ear pressed against the closed office door, trying to overhear what's going on.

"Again," Mia begs, wriggling her butt at me and pushing back on my fingers. "Spank me again."

A groan spills out from Landon's lips. "Fuck me," he says. "You will be the death of us, Mia." He unzips his pants, and his cock jumps out.

Mia squirms and licks her lips as Landon positions himself by her head. "Open your mouth," he orders.

My cock hardens as she parts her lips and delicately drags her tongue across Landon's head. A shudder runs through his body as she hollows her cheeks and sucks him. I never thought of myself as a voyeur, but watching Mia take Landon down her throat almost makes me blow my load.

I grab the bottle of lube and smooth some over my fingers. Parting her ass cheeks, I rub the lube in circles around her puckered anus, slowly, gently. She moans into Landon's cock and thrusts her butt back toward me. Goosebumps erupt on her skin, and she shivers as I play with her bud.

She likes this.

Steadily, I push in the tip of my forefinger into her tight passage before adding a second one. She whimpers and clenches, squeezing my fingers in a vise-like grip. "It feels so weird," she groans, pulling her mouth free of Landon's cock and turning her head around to look at me.

"Wrap your pretty little lips around Landon's dick," I order her. She wants forceful, she said. Even now, her eyes are bright with heat, and her pussy is wet and swollen. She's absolutely soaked.

She shivers as I drag a fingertip through her dripping slit. Her legs part wider, and she tilts her head back toward Landon, her mouth falling open, her hand reaching for his cock. She strains against my fingers, her muscles quivering and clenching as I spread her juices over her clitoris and tease that pulsing nub.

Her breathing quickens as she approaches the edge. Normally, I love watching Mia orgasm. Today, I pull my fingers away before she can climax, and move my attention back to her tightly puckered anus.

Mia groans again as I slowly work two fingers into her tight ass. I push deeper, and she instinctively clenches before making herself relax. "How does it feel?" I ask her. "Any pain?"

She removes her mouth from Landon's cock and shakes her head. "It feels strange," she mutters. "Strange and weird and good."

"You want this, don't you? You want to take my cock up your ass. Isn't that right, Mia?"

Her cheeks flame, but I'm not letting her off the hook. After this weekend, I know that sweet little Mia likes dirty talk. She might blush and stammer, but her pussy gives her away. She's drenched. "Tell me you want it."

"I do," she whispers. "I want it."

"You want what, Mia?" Drizzling more lube over her, I press my forefinger and middle finger into her virgin ass again. She's so tight. I smooth the gel into her passage, moving my fingers back and forth, scissoring her open.

She gasps. Landon grips her hair and tugs her closer. "That's it," he purrs. "Take me all the way, baby. Keep your eyes on me. I want you to look at me when you suck me off. I want to see your eyes glaze as you take my entire length in your mouth." He strokes her cheek, the movement gentle. "See what you do to me, baby," he groans, clenching his eyes shut with pleasure.

It's time. I coat the butt plug liberally with lube and position it against her ass. "Don't tighten up," I warn her. "I have all the time in the world, baby. You're going to take this plug for me today."

It's a total lie—we have clients arriving in an hour. Landon's the lucky prick today who gets to come. I'm going to have to nurse a case of blue balls all afternoon.

I push the plug against her steadily, my fingers working her clitoris at the same time. Landon caresses her face. "It feels good, doesn't it, baby?" he says, coaxing her to relax.

She nods, her eyes wild with need. She's very close. I increase the pressure on her clitoris, pressing down on her, and she explodes. Her muscles tighten. Her pussy clenches my fingers and her entire body trembles and spasms. Landon's fingers tighten their grip in her hair. His body goes rigid as he empties into her mouth with a shout.

Again, I'm really glad about the fired receptionist.

Her orgasm goes on and on. I'm relentless. My fingers thrust into her pussy, and at the same time, I push the plug into her, inch by inch, until it's seated between her ass cheeks.

"No more," she gasps out finally. "Please Ben, I'm too sensitive." She slumps on the desk, a soft sheen of sweat covering her skin.

Landon collapses into my chair. "How does the plug feel?" he asks her.

"Full." Her cheeks color. "I've never been so turned on in my life." She gives us an embarrassed laugh. "I think I like it."

I smile at her ruefully. "I want to hear all about how much you like it," I start, "but we have clients arriving here. As much as I want to fuck you on my desk, I'm afraid I'm going to have to throw you out."

"We have clients?" Landon gives me a dismayed look and reaches for his phone. "Damn it, you're right."

I give Mia a cautious gaze, afraid we might have offended her, but she just chuckles, surveying the mess. "I knocked the photos off the desk," she says. "I didn't even notice."

She moves to pick them up, and her mouth forms a little O of surprise. "Plug moving in your ass?" I grin.

"Yes." She takes a few more steps, and my cock stiffens further. "Well, this is going to be an interesting walk back to my store." She picks the photo frames off the floor and sets them back on my desk. "Why do you have pictures of all these babies at your desk?" she asks curiously.

"They're babies of our patients," I reply. "A lot of our clients were ready to give up on their marriages, and their love lives when they came to see us." I smile at Annie Landry's chubby newborn daughter. "This is the reason we do what we do."

She gives me a strange look and then she hugs me. "What's that for?" I ask her, surprised.

"No reason." A grin tugs at her lips. "Can't I hug the guy who just shoved something the size of a giant cucumber up my ass?"

I roll my eyes. "Don't exaggerate; it's nowhere as big as that."

We help her get dressed, then I spray some air freshener since the office reeks of sex. "Hey," I remember when she's almost at the door. "I was going to ask you. Do you know someone who might want to be our receptionist? We need someone trustworthy and discreet."

"In other words, the exact opposite of Amy Cooke?" She frowns thoughtfully. "I can't think of anyone off the top of my head, but I'll give it some thought." She pulls her phone out of her purse and glances at the time. "Okay, I better go. See you guys later?"

I pull her into my arms and kiss her, hard and insistent. Mia has me feeling like a randy teenager. I almost want to cancel all our clients this afternoon and spend the day savoring her sweet body. "Enjoy the plug," I say into her ear. "And if you're going to masturbate when you get to your store, call us and ask for permission first."

"Ooh, bossy," she says with a grin as she pulls herself free. "I like it."

16

MIA

I walk back to my shop in tiny, mincing steps. With each move I make, the butt plug shifts in my ass. It feels so weird, so forbidden, and it's turning me on. My entire body tingles with desire, and my panties are soaked.

As soon as I get back, I promise myself that I'll make myself come. I'll call Ben and Landon to ask for permission. Maybe I'll even keep them on the line and let them hear my moans and sighs of pleasure. There's a smile on my lips as I imagine their reaction. I can picture Ben in his tidy office, Landon in his messier one, their cocks straining against the fabric of their trousers. I can almost see the desire on their faces as they stroke themselves.

I've never been brave enough to have phone sex, but today, I feel invincible.

I'm turning the corner on Water and Main when I run into Amy Cooke. My lust immediately fizzles out. Running into the former cheerleader is surefire ladywood killer.

Hoping to get by her without being forced into a conversation, I nod politely at the woman and try to keep walking.

Unfortunately, Amy's in a chatty mood. No, scratch that. She's in an accusing mood. She comes to a dead halt outside the China Garden and points a finger at me. "You," she exclaims dramatically. "You hussy."

I smell Maggie Zhang's spring rolls. Mmm. The idea of takeout sounds pretty appealing, even with a plug up my ass and Amy wagging her forefinger in my face.

"Hello Amy," I say neutrally. "How've you been?"

"You whore." Her voice shakes with barely suppressed anger. Amy's always had a dramatic side, and she's been known to fly off the rails at the slightest provocation. Like right now. "Because of you, Landon West fired me."

I narrow my eyes at her. When I was younger, I'd go out of my way to avoid Amy and Tiffany and their cheerleader friends, but I'm not in high school anymore, and the great thing about growing up is realizing that you don't have to kiss the butt of the popular kids anymore. "I'm pretty sure they fired you because you're a horrible gossip," I tell her, my tone steely. "Now, if you'll excuse me..."

"Please," she scoffs. "They fired me because I knew they were sleeping with a patient. You." She sneers at me. "Good little Mia Gardner, having a threesome with her therapists. They can get their license suspended for what they did, you know."

My patience, already fraying, snaps. "I'm not their patient," I hiss out through clenched teeth. I think about the photos of all those adorable smiling babies that adorn Ben's office, of the pride in Landon's voice when he talks about the work they do. Ben and Landon help people, something petty, vicious Amy Cooke can never understand. "I've never been their patient, which you'd know if you were a better receptionist."

I take a deep breath. I almost never lose my temper, but

I'm well and truly in a rage now. "You don't give a shit about the work they do. Dr. West and Dr. Long are good people, and they care about their patients. Unlike you. You're a selfish, trouble-making bitch, who only cares about herself."

Amy looks at something over my shoulder, and her expression turns nervous. "You're going to pay for this," she says in a low voice. "All of you." Then she hurries away.

My heart races in my chest. My palms feel sweaty as the adrenaline leaves my body, and my body starts to tremble. I frown at Amy's sudden departure. I thought for sure that she'd have more to say.

Then an arm circles my waist, and Landon kisses my cheek. "That was very sweet of you," he says, his eyes tender. "If we weren't in public, I'd kiss you."

I turn around and see Ben a half-step behind, holding my phone in his hand. "You left this at our office," he says. "We were just coming to give it back to you when we heard your confrontation with Amy."

"Are you angry with me?" I ask hesitantly. I shouldn't have lost my temper. Amy has a mean and vindictive side to her. I shouldn't have fought back. Landon and Ben fired her, and I called her a selfish trouble-making bitch. I think about what she said. *You're going to pay for this, all of you.* "I'm sorry."

"Angry with you?" Ben takes my hand in his. "Mia, I'm touched that you came to our defense the way you did. You fought for us. That means a lot to me."

"We had a loud argument in the middle of the street." I look around at the restaurants and shops all around us. There's China Garden. The barber shop. The Merry Cocka-too. I had a screaming match with Amy Cooke in the heart of downtown New Summit. A screaming match in which

Amy accused me, at top volume, of sleeping with Landon and Ben.

I feel a little faint. "Anyone could have heard us," I whisper in horror. "Maggie Zhang. Mr. Potter. Nina. Anyone passing by."

"Yet your first instinct was to defend us." There's an unusual warmth in Landon's expression. "Not to protect your reputation."

I flush at the way they're looking at me. As if I was some kind of hero. "I couldn't let her throw around accusations about you," I mutter, looking at my sandals. "She said you could lose your licenses."

Ben shakes his head. "You're not our patient," he says emphatically. "We've done nothing wrong. We have nothing to worry about." His voice turns low. "Let me prove it to you. Have dinner with us tonight at the Chapman Inn."

I look up in surprise. The Chapman Inn is an old historic hotel on the water. Rooms cost hundreds of dollars a night, and their restaurant is very fancy. I've never been in there.

Am I ready for this? If I go to dinner with Landon and Ben, then tomorrow morning, everyone in New Summit will know. Add in Amy's allegations, and I might as well print a 'Mia is having a threesome' headline in the Summit Star.

I bite my lower lip nervously. This feels significant. This feels like Ben and Landon are publicly acknowledging our unconventional relationship. Do I have the courage to do the same?

I'm making a list in my head of all the reasons I should say yes.

1. Ben and Landon just asked me to recommend a receptionist, someone trustworthy. Which means

they trust me and value my judgment. Dennis, on the other hand, referred to me as a girl who owns a dress store.

2. They listened to what I wanted sexually, without judgment or reservations, and made it come true.
3. The earth-shattering orgasms.

Yes, it's unconventional. Yes, I'm going to be New Summit's biggest scandal, even bigger than the time when Dulcie Thompson ran off with Paul Scott the day before her wedding with Jared Kane, and she didn't even return the wedding presents.

I could say no and end this thing with Ben and Landon. But I don't want to. I think back on the passionless year I spent with Dennis. Of the trapped feeling in my chest when he proposed at the Miller Tavern (New Summit's second-best restaurant, on a Monday night, because the steak dinner was half-price.) Of the secret relief I felt when I'd seen him cheating with Tiffany Slater.

I don't want to go back to that version of me. The version that cared more about what other people thought of her, and less about her own happiness.

I'm aware that I'm having this epiphany in the middle of downtown, outside China Garden with its oh-so-tempting-spring rolls, with a plug up my butt. Cassie's right. Aliens have swooped in and replaced old-Mia with a new, improved version. I like it.

"I'd love to have dinner with you."

Smiles break out on both their faces. "Excellent," Landon says. "We'll pick you up at seven."

Ben grins wickedly. "And Mia?" he says, stepping closer to me and leaning in so only I can hear what he says. "Wear the plug and no panties. We have plans for you after dinner."

"Yes, Dr. Long," I reply meekly, though I'm sure I spoil the effect by winking at them. "I'm looking forward to dessert."

17

LANDON

My dad cheated on my mom their entire marriage, and I swore I'd never be that person. I've avoided relationships throughout my adult life because I've secretly been terrified that I won't stay faithful.

But things feel different with Mia. With Mia, I want to try. When I saw her confront Amy and defend Ben and me, I knew, with certainty, that I could never do anything to hurt this woman.

Unlike most people, I've never been invested in traditions. Ben picked an old Victorian to renovate; I tore down the wreck on my lot and built a modern wood and glass house in its place. A threesome is a lot more complicated than a house, but the principle still holds. I'm comfortable with unconventional relationships.

And Ben? I think it's fair to say that Mia's had a positive effect on my friend. He dated that strung-out lawyer for six months, and I don't think she spent the night at his house once. He claims it's because Becky was messy and would disrupt his routine, but that was just an excuse.

With Mia, Ben's cooking meals. Letting the dishes pile up in his sink and savoring the company instead of rushing away to clean. When she dropped her panties on the floor of his bedroom, he didn't pick them up with a disapproving look.

I'm pretty sure Ben wants to date her too.

"So we're going public," Ben says to me as we walk back to work. "You have to tell Sophia."

Right. My sister. I've never pretended to be a saint around Sophia, but I have no idea how she's going to take this news. She's trying to fit into this town. If her new friends decide they're going to disapprove of our threesome, then Sophia's going to be forced to take sides.

Can I do that to my sister?

"Landon." Ben notices my expression of consternation, and he rolls his eyes. "Sophia's not a child. She's a lot more observant than you give her credit for. You spent most of the weekend with Mia and me. I'm pretty sure she already has a good idea what's going on."

I hope he's right. Because otherwise, I'm about to have the most awkward conversation in the world.

Later that afternoon, I sit in my living room, waiting for Sophia to get back from school. I'm a nervous wreck at the thought of telling my only living relative, and it makes me appreciate Mia even more. She's a lot stronger than she appears. I was attracted to her from the moment I laid eyes on her, but spending time with her, I've learned she's much more than a pretty face and a smoking body.

Her parents wanted her to go work at a bank when she graduated. They'd even lined up a job for her, but Mia was passionate about fashion, so she struck out on her own, borrowing money from Cassie to open her store. She's been open for five years, and she's already paid back her loan and is saving money so she can buy her building from George Bollington. "He's hurting for money," she said to us the day we went sailing. "I have a ten-year lease, and he can't increase my rent, but he's charging Nina well above market rate. It's a perfect location for the Merry Cockatoo, but still." She'd shaken her head wryly. "There's a rumor going around that Starbucks is sniffing around looking for a location in downtown New Summit. I'm sure Dr. Bollington would love to kick me out and sell to them."

The front door opens, and Sophia walks in. Her eyebrows rise when she sees me sitting on the couch. I'm not usually home when she comes back from school. "Hey Landon," she greets me cheerfully. "You're back early today."

"Yeah." I clear my throat. "I have something I need to tell you."

"You're in a threesome," she replies, laughing when she sees my expression. "Landon, this place is crazy. Penny's sister Alexis was having an early lunch at the China Garden, and she heard Amy Cooke and Mia Gardner have a screaming match outside. Of course, Alexis being who she is, she texted Penny right away, who immediately asked me if I knew about it."

"And?" I ask her warily. "Are you cool with this?"

Sophia shrugs. "It's your life, Landon. If you're happy, I'm happy." Her lips curl into a grin. "Penny's heartbroken. She has a crush on you. I have to listen to Landon-this, and Landon-that, and oh-my-God-Sophia-is-it-true-that-Landon-has-a-tattoo-of-a-dragon-on-his-inner-thigh?" She puts a finger in her throat and makes a gagging noise. "Maybe she'll stop now."

I laugh at the expression of disgust on her face. "What'd you tell her about the tattoo?"

"That it wasn't a dragon but a mouse."

"Hey," I say, offended. "I'll have you know... never mind. You want to meet Mia sometime?"

"I'd love that. Is she nice?"

"She's pretty awesome."

"Good." Sophia plops herself down on the couch and rests her head on my shoulder. "I'm really happy for you, Landon. Oh hey, I forgot to tell you. I got the job. You're looking at the Merry Cockatoo's newest line cook. Nina has me on the weekend lunch shift to start."

"Congratulations, kiddo."

"Right back at you." We sit in silence for a while, and then she gets to her feet. "I'm starving," she says. "You staying home for dinner tonight? I can make something."

I shake my head. "Mia, Ben, and I are going to the Chapman Inn for dinner."

She whistles. "Fancy," she says. "This girl must be good for you. It's not often that you cut loose. Oh, that reminds me. Can you get me an order of their house salad to go, with the dressing on the side? I want to try and replicate the recipe."

"Of the salad?"

She looks at me as if I'm a dim-witted child. "I'm trying to replicate the salad dressing recipe, Landon."

"Consider it done."

18

BENJAMIN

We pick Mia up promptly at seven. She looks glorious tonight. She's wearing a deep red cocktail dress. Her hair is sleek and shiny, pulled back into a ponytail at the nape of her neck. She looks *kissable*.

"You look fantastic," I tell her.

Her eyes shine with excitement. "You look pretty good yourself," she says, openly staring at the two of us. "Very hot."

Landon laughs. "Shall we?"

The Chapman Inn is set on the outskirts of New Summit. It's a twenty-minute drive. Landon and I tossed to see whose car we'd take, and I lost, so I'm driving. I help Mia into my Porsche, and Landon folds himself into the narrow, cramped backseat. "Nice car," she remarks as she gets in.

I don't reply at once. I'm distracted by the way her dress rides up her thighs. "Are you wearing panties?" I ask her sternly.

"You'll have to check," she replies airily. "Maybe I am. Maybe I'm not."

"Really?" I slant her a look.

Her lips twitch. "Yes, really. And if I've failed to obey your orders, I'm going to get a spanking, right?"

Landon chuckles. "Bad girls don't get spanked," he tells her as I shift into first and move the car forward. "Spanking is a reward, not a punishment, Mia."

A thought strikes me. We drive out of town, and about ten minutes into our journey, I take a turn off the main road into an unpaved country road, wincing as the gravel rattles against the undercarriage of my car. Still, this is going to be worth it.

"Where are we going?" Mia asks as I slow the car to a halt. "We're not there yet, are we?"

I turn toward her with a smirk. "We're halfway there. Get out of the car. Landon and I need to check if you followed instructions."

Her lips part and her breathing catches. "Here?"

We've come to a stop under a tree. The sky is overcast, the sun hidden behind a thick cover of clouds. "There's no one around." I get out of the car and walk around to open the passenger door for her. "Come on, Mia. Bend over the trunk."

It's a Porsche. The rear end of my car is a gentle curve, so Mia doesn't bend over as much as she leans over. Without being told, she spreads her legs about shoulder-width apart. Our sweet, good girl is turned on.

Landon crouches behind Mia. He slides a hand up her leg, teasingly slow. She gasps as he lifts the skirt of her dress out of the way, and she feels the cool evening air on her naked flesh.

"No panties." I can see the base of the butt plug poking out from between her round ass cheeks.

Her skin is creamy and soft, and as the two of us look,

she wriggles her butt. "You promised me a spanking if I was good," she points out, turning her head to look at us.

"Let's add patience to that," Landon suggests. "You need to be good and patient."

She pouts adorably. I can't resist. I spank that curvy ass, and she moans and bites her lip in response.

Landon runs his hands over her. "I'm going to take you tonight," he says into her ear. His fingers close over the butt plug and he twists it around.

Mia throws her head back, her eyes shut, her face etched with pleasure. I explore the folds of her pussy. She's drenched. "You like the plug, honey?" I ask her.

She nods wordlessly. I place my fingers at her lips. "Suck," I order. She flushes, but opens her mouth and licks her juices off my fingers. My dick hardens as her tongue pokes out. God, she's a wet dream.

"We should go." Landon's voice is reluctant. "We do have dinner reservations."

"Yeah." Mia sighs in disappointment then gives us a hopeful look. "Maybe we can stop at this spot on a different day and continue where we left off."

I chuckle and kiss her hard. I feel like the luckiest guy in the world.

19

MIA

I feel a little sorry for Ben and Landon as we pull into the parking lot of the Chapman Inn. They're both still sporting erections. I grin as they adjust themselves in the car. "Ready to eat?" I smirk at them.

Landon shakes his head. "Brat."

We walk inside, and the hostess seats us right away at a secluded table in the corner. "Wow, this place is nice," I tell them, looking around with wide eyes. The restaurant is on the ground floor of the inn. Windows look out to the beautifully landscaped garden, filled with blooming flowers. The tables are covered with white damask tablecloths, and vases of pink roses add decorative touches. The lighting is dim and romantic, and classical music plays in the background. "Have you been here before?"

They shake their heads. "There's never been anyone I cared about enough to bring here," Ben says, his expression serious. "Until now."

"Really?" My heart beats faster. Outside China Garden this morning, I decided I was ready to take a risk on them, but I had no idea how they felt. Now, hope trickles through me. It seems impossible that two men this attractive could want me. I want to pinch myself.

"Really," Landon confirms. He's about to say something else when the waiter shows up to take our drink orders. Landon orders a bottle of wine. Once we're alone again, he looks at me, his eyes hooded. "Can you feel the plug in your ass?"

I nod wordlessly. I've been trying hard to ignore it, but every time I shift in my seat, the plug moves inside me. I feel filled, and it's driving me crazy with lust. "I know it's the Chapman Inn," I whisper, "but I can't wait to get back home."

Ben's lips lift in a smile. "So impatient," he teases. "We're not going anywhere, Mia. What's the rush?"

Our wine arrives, and we order dinner. Conversation flows easily between us. We don't talk about anything too serious, but things feel different. I can tell by the way they look at me, the way they touch me.

"Can I ask you something?" Landon asks when there's a break in the conversation. He leans forward and refills my glass. Ben, who's driving, waves the bottle away when Landon tilts it in his direction.

"Sure," I reply hesitantly.

"If we were to ask you to date both of us," he says, "would you say yes?"

A wide smile breaks out on my face. "You don't know New Summit at all, do you?" I tease them. "If I didn't want to date you, I'd have never come here for dinner. Tomorrow morning, the entire town will be gossiping about the three of us."

"And you're okay with it?"

I take a deep breath. To be honest, I'm nervous. When I'm with Landon and Ben, I have a great time. I want to be with them, but the idea of being judged by the entire town scares me. I've been Good-Girl-Mia all my life. Now, I'm going to become Slut-Mia. "It can't be helped."

Ben gives me an intent look. "If you want to keep our relationship private, that's okay," he reassures me. "I'm an outsider here. I don't care what the town thinks about me, but you've lived among these people your whole life. We want you to feel comfortable."

"Is that okay?" I exhale in relief.

"Of course, Mia," Landon replies. "We care about you. We want you to be happy."

I bite my lip. "I care about you too," I say, looking both of them in the eye. In such a short period, only a few days, these two men have become really, *really* important to me. "Thank you for being so understanding."

Just then, a shrill voice cuts through the hushed atmosphere. "I told you," Amy Cooke shrieks, barging into the quiet restaurant with George Bollington at her side, and Dennis just a half-step behind her. Dennis? What the heck is he doing here?

The trio marches up to our table. "See?" Amy crows, turning to my frowning landlord. "Look at the three of them." Her voice lowers to an accusing hush. "Dr. Bollington? Mia Gardner is a patient of Dr. Long and Dr. West, and they're in a ménage a trois."

She pronounces ménage like manage. I'd laugh if I weren't so mortified. Every single person in the restaurant has stopped eating and is staring at the three of us.

"Is that true?" Dennis has an expression of shock on his face. "Mia? You're fucking both of them? I could believe this of Cassie, but you?"

"What's that supposed to mean? You can believe it of Cassie, but not me?"

He looks discomfited. My landlord cuts in. "Is that relevant?" he demands. "Well, West, Long, is this true? Are the three of you sexually involved?"

So much for keeping our relationship private until I was ready for the gossip. Thank you, Amy Cooke. I hope you get a yeast infection.

"Yes," I admit. "We are, not that it's anyone's business." I glare at Amy and Dennis. "But Ben and Landon have never been my psychotherapists. Amy is lying."

"No, I'm not," Amy insists. "I was there when Mia came to see them."

"For a consultation," Landon interjects, his tone tight with anger. "And she decided not to pursue treatment with us. The College guidelines are quite clear. There's no issue here."

"For you, maybe. Ms. Gardner is, however, in violation of her lease." George Bollington turns to me. "This relationship of yours," he spits out, "is an abomination. There's a morality clause in your lease, Mia, and you're in violation of it. You have thirty days to vacate your premises."

I look at him, shocked. I'm being evicted.

20

LANDON

Ben and I get rid of Bollington, Amy, and Mia's sniveling ex. Once they're out of there, I turn to Mia, who's trembling.

Her lips quiver and her eyes fill with tears, but she brushes them away. "Mia, honey, don't worry. Bollington's just being an asshole. He can't evict you for being in a threesome. That's flagrantly illegal. No court in the country will allow him to get away with it."

She sniffs. "I can't afford to take him to court, Landon. Lawyers are expensive." She sighs and picks at her food. "Yeah, I know that morality clause is probably garbage, but what can I do? He's got all the power, and I have none. That's just the way the world works."

Ben puts a hand on her forearm. "I promise you," he says intently. "We will fix this. Please don't worry, Mia. Let us handle your landlord for you. Please don't let this ruin our evening."

She smiles at us tremulously. "Okay."

We eat the rest of our meal in silence, our evening ruined. In the car on the way back, I clear my throat and turn to face her in the back seat, where she's insisted on sitting. "Do you want us to drop you off at home?" I ask her, hoping she'll say no. I want Mia. I don't just want to have sex with her. I want to feel her soft body curled up between us, and in the morning, I want to wake up next to her.

Her lips curve into a wicked smile, and she spreads her legs, slowly hiking her skirt up, and exposing her bare pussy. "No," she says, her fingers snaking down to the cleft between her legs. "I was promised sex."

Ben glances in the rearview mirror, and the car almost goes off the road. "For heaven's sake, Mia. Are you trying to kill us?"

"I'm sorry." She flutters her eyelashes at us, the little minx. "Are you having trouble concentrating on the road?"

I chuckle. "Payback's a bitch, honey," I tell her. "I hope you know what you're getting into."

21

MIA

We make our way to Ben's bedroom. The moment I walk in, Landon pushes me on the bed. "You've been a very naughty girl, Mia," he says, his eyes gleaming with wicked lust. "I should put you over my knee and spank you."

Ben settles himself in the leather armchair, his legs stretched out. From the look of heat in his eyes, he's going to enjoy watching this. A shiver of arousal runs through me at the idea of being spanked by Landon while Ben watches.

"You like that, don't you?" Landon sits on the edge of the bed, wraps an arm around my waist, and pulls me over his lap. He lifts my skirt out of the way and smacks my ass. "You like the idea of Ben watching you get punished."

"I do," I moan. The sharp sting fades, and my pussy feels hot and heavy with need.

Ben surveys me with a tilt of his head. His cock is a hard ridge against his fly, and I press my thighs together as a wave of lust goes through me. "Beg Landon to spank you again," he commands.

I bite my lip. They're right. I am a naughty, naughty girl.

"Please spank me, Landon," I whimper. Landon's fingers skim over the curve of my ass. His hands spread my legs apart, exposing me to Ben's appreciative gaze.

"So beautiful," Ben mutters, his voice thick with desire.

Landon's fingers explore my folds. He slides a finger into my pussy, and groans as he finds me soaked. He taps the base of the butt plug, and I shiver as I feel it move inside me. "How does it feel?"

It feels like they've been torturing me for days, teasing and tormenting me with overwhelming pleasure. This morning, they bent me over Ben's desk at work and pushed a butt plug into my ass. All day, I've been wandering around in a fog of arousal. Even when Amy, Dennis, and Dr. Bollington were creating the scene, I was conscious of the plug.

Now, it's going to be replaced by a steel-hard cock. I can't wait. My nipples harden with desire; my skin prickles with anticipation.

"All day I've wanted you, Mia," Ben growls. "All fucking day. Every time I looked at my desk, I got hard." There's an undertone of laughter in his voice. "Do you have any idea how awkward it is to see clients when you have a raging boner?"

Landon's palm descends on my ass. "I think you should be punished for that," he purrs. His fingers close around the plug that's embedded in my ass, and he pulls it out slowly.

I feel my body stretch to accommodate the widest part of the plug before he pushes it back in again. My nerve endings blaze with fire. My entire body trembles. I cannot believe I'm going to do this. My long-held secret fantasies brought to life by these two amazing men.

I'm a lucky, lucky girl. Even if I lose the lease to my store, I won't regret my relationship with Landon and Ben.

Landon alternates spanks of my ass with tugs of the plug. Occasionally, his fingers slide down my cleft, teasing my clitoris.

While Landon spanks me, Ben unzips his fly. His massive cock springs free. He fists himself, and I can't pull my gaze free.

Landon shoves two fingers into my drenched pussy. I whimper and squirm on his lap. "Please," I beg. He's so close to my clitoris. I've been aching all evening. I've been at the edge for hours, waiting for them to push me over.

"What do you think, Ben?" Landon pretends to consider. "Do you think Mia deserves to come?"

Ben's lips lift into a smile. "She has been a very bad girl," he says, winking at me. "But I'm in a generous mood." His hand pumps his cock, and he throws his head back.

Landon's fingers circle over my clitoris. Each touch makes me quiver, bringing me relentlessly closer to my orgasm. I bite my lip. My entire body tingles and tightens; every muscle clenches as a familiar heat begins to coil in my core.

I've had a lot of steamy fantasies. This beats every single one of them.

Then Ben rises to his feet and stalks toward me. His cock bobs at my lips and I open my mouth gladly, aching to taste him. His fingers grip my hair, and he slides into my mouth, hard and deep.

Landon's stroking me faster now. With his spare hand, he's tugging at the plug in my ass. It's all too much. Ben's hard cock in my mouth. Landon's fingers on my clitoris. I can't take it anymore.

Then a dam bursts, and I scream. Wave after wave of release flood through me. I sink my nails into Ben's hips as I flail on Landon's lap. He doesn't stop. He keeps going, wrenching every last bit of pleasure from me, until I finally collapse on the bed, wrung out, drained, and sated.

They give me a minute. My pussy is puffy and swollen, but I'm greedy. I want them again.

We get naked, clothing flying all over the room. Landon lies down on the bed and beckons me. "Come sit on my cock, Mia."

I blush at his frank description. A shiver of lust runs through my body as I climb on the bed and crawl over to Landon on my hands and knees.

The mattress shifts as Ben climbs on the bed as well. His hands rub my shoulders from behind, and he wraps his arms around me. His warm breath sounds against my ear. "I want you," he says. His thumb brushes a lock of my hair from my cheek. "I want to fuck your pretty little ass."

Landon reaches for me. He's rolled on a condom while Ben was nuzzling my neck, and now, he positions me over his steel-hard cock. His head brushes at my slit, teasing me a little before he pulls me down on him.

I gasp as he thrusts into me. His thick length fills me, stretching my muscles. "God, your pussy is so fucking tight," Landon groans, as he rolls his hips upward.

I'm too lost in my haze of lust to respond. Landon's large cock is in my pussy, and the thick plug is in my ass, and I've never felt more completely possessed.

"Bend forward," Ben instructs from behind me, his voice ragged with need. He pulls the plug free, and liberally coats his cock with lubricant. Fresh lube is drizzled on my tight bud, and I inhale sharply.

Ben grins at me. "Remember to breathe, Mia." His hands wrap around my waist. "I'll be gentle," he says, his voice soothing and calm. "We'll take it slow. You have nothing to be nervous about."

Nervous? I'm not shivering from nerves. I'm shaking with anticipation.

Landon tugs at my swollen nipples, pinching them between his thumb and forefinger before pulling me forward and taking them between his teeth. His sucks and nibbles.

My pulse pounds. The blood roars in my ears. I'm painfully aroused.

Ben lines the head of his cock up with my asshole. He kisses my shoulder and pushes forward, steady and firm. My passage yields to him, and his head is in.

My mouth forms a wide O of surprise. Though I was looking forward to this moment, I'd been bracing myself for pain. This, however, isn't painful. It's overwhelming and intense, but the plug in my ass all day has prepared me for Ben.

"Fuck." Landon's eyes clench shut. "Your pussy just gripped my cock. Oh my God, Mia, you're so fucking tight."

Ben gives me some time to get used to his girth, then he pulls out almost completely, and slides in again. This time, I can't hold back my gasp of pleasure. "So good," I sigh, my fingers gripping the pillowcases on either side of Landon's head.

Ben strokes in and out of me, shallow strokes that leave me aching for more. "Mia," he grinds out, his fingers digging into my waist. "I'm not going to last." A shiver runs through him.

Landon kisses me possessively. His thumb teases my tender nipples. "We're going to fuck you now, Mia," he says. There's a burning intensity in his gaze, and I can tell that he's hanging on to control by a thread. "We're going to fuck you deep and hard."

"Yes," I hiss. I feel like I'm under a spell. I feel lightheaded. All the blood has left my brain and pooled in my pussy and ass. My clitoris throbs, greedily begging for more attention. "Do it."

Fire blazes in Landon's eyes. He nods to Ben, and then he lifts me up, almost pulling his cock out of my pussy. Ben pulls out too. Then, with perfect synchronicity, they slam into me.

Hard.

Deep.

Powerful.

I whimper as they pound into me with long, punishing strokes. How could I have ever been content with Dennis' inept fumbling? I want to thank Tiffany Slater. Had I never found the two of them on my ex-fiancé's dining table, I'd have never found the courage to break it off with him. I'd have never met Landon and Ben.

That thought is terrifying.

I didn't know I needed to be taken this way. I twist and flail between their hard bodies. My muscles start to clench, and heat twists in my core. Sweat slicks our bodies. Their breathing is harsh as they stroke in and out of my pussy and ass.

They set a rhythm going. When one of them pulls out, the other pushes in. Ben's hands grip my hips and my ass.

"I'm close," Landon clenches out, his fingers trailing a path down to my pussy. He finds my clitoris with unerring precision, and he pinches that swollen nub.

It's too much. The pressure has been building, and his touch sets me off. I shriek as I climax. Ben growls a curse, and his grip on me tightens as he finds his release. Landon's only a half-step behind.

"Wow," I manage. I'm exhausted. I feel boneless and drained, but I've never been happier. "That was better than my fantasy." I grin happily at both of them. "When can we do that again?"

Landon groans and a smile creases Ben's face. "We've created a monster." He pulls me into his arms, and I curl up between the two of them, savoring the warmth of their bodies.

Whatever happens tomorrow, I'm ready.

22

BENJAMIN

Early the next morning, Landon and I slip out of bed before Mia can wake up, and we head to George Bollington's office.

He looks warily at us when we walk in. "I've made up my mind about Ms. Gardner's lease," he says without preamble. "I'm not going to change it."

"Yes, you are," Landon replies, equally bluntly. "My father wasn't much of a human being, but he taught me one very important lesson. The secret of every successful negotiation is to realize that everyone wants something." He gives Bollington a steady look. "What will it take for you to stop harassing Mia?"

Bollington steeples his fingers. "I told you," he says weakly. "I've made my decision."

I look at the man in front of us. Sweat beads on his brow and his eyes dart around the room, looking anywhere but at the two of us. Bollington isn't as inflexible as he sounds.

He wants something.

"No you haven't." I take a seat opposite the man and look

at him steadily. "If you'd really intended to evict Mia, you'd ask us to leave. So, what is it? What's it going to take?"

"Fine," he snaps. "Leave town, and I'll leave your girl-friend alone."

Landon shakes his head. "That option isn't on the table," he replies, his voice hard. "Play ball with us, Bollington. Mia doesn't have money to fight the eviction, but we do. If we have to throw an army of lawyers at you, we will."

The older man squirms in his chair, but doesn't say anything.

I think hard. What's the endpoint here? Sure, we can take Bollington to court, but he's Mia's landlord as well as a prominent New Summit citizen. I don't care if he's my enemy, but I don't want to make Mia's life any more difficult than it needs to be. Already, she's going to be the target of wagging tongues.

Bollington wanted us to leave town. While it might be because we're sex therapists, I'd wager it has a lot more to do with the fact that we're competition. We're poaching clients from him.

Then I remember what Mia said the day we went sailing. She mentioned Bollington was over-extended. He's hurting for money, she'd said.

I have to tread warily. If I offer money directly, I could risk offending the man. Bollington places a lot of pride on appearances. He wants to be perceived as successful and powerful, no matter what the underlying truth is.

"Would you consider renegotiating Mia's lease?" I ask carefully.

"What do you mean?" He looks up, a glimmer of hope in his eyes, and I know I've hit pay dirt.

"It's not unheard of for a tenant to pay to amend a lease," I reply. "We'd like that morality clause removed, and we're willing to make it worth your while." I tilt my head to one side and wonder how much money to offer. Mia's rent is probably three grand a month. Starbucks might pay five grand. "Say a hundred thousand dollars?"

I can see him do the math in his head, his eyes greedy. "Make it one twenty-five, and we have a deal," he counters.

Landon's eyes narrow. "Tell you what," he says smoothly. "We'll make it one fifty, but in two payments. Half of it right now, half in a year."

That's clever. I don't trust Bollington; he might take the money and harass Mia in a thousand petty ways. This way, he's got something at stake.

I can see Bollington visibly hesitate, then the amount of cash at stake sinks in. "Okay," he says. "It's a deal."

I smile in satisfaction. Excellent. One problem down. The next step: warning Mia's ex to stay out of her business.

23

MIA

When I wake up, the bedroom is empty, and Landon and Ben are nowhere to be seen. Good. I need to talk to my landlord.

I've tossed and turned all night long, unable to sleep, but this morning, I've reached a decision. I'm not going to let Dr. Bollington get away with this. What I do with my personal life is none of his business. The morality clause was intended so that I don't sell sex toys in my store. It wasn't intended to control me.

Last night, I'd been too upset at the scene that Amy and Dennis created at the Chapman Inn. Ben and Landon had gone to the trouble of taking me out for a special meal, and the two of them had ruined it. I was ready to give in.

This morning, I'm not quite as compliant. This morning, I'm ready to fight back.

I march over to North Street, to the converted yellow brick row house where George Bollington sees patients. Ashley, his receptionist, looks up when I come in. "Is he in?" I demand.

She barely looks up from her phone, Candy Crush

claiming most of her attention. "It's been busy this morning," she says. "It's almost never busy around here. Yeah, he's here. Go on in."

I turn the handle of George Bollington's inner office. He's sitting at his desk, reading the latest issue of the Summit Star. He looks up as I enter. "Mia," he says flatly. "What a surprise."

I hold up my hand. Amy's flair for the dramatic must have rubbed off on me. "Before you can threaten me again," I tell him, "I must warn you that I'm done being a pushover." I give expression to years of pent-up frustration. I can't have lingerie displays. My mannequins are too sexy. The clothes I sell are too slutty. I can't host viewing parties in my store, and I certainly can't serve wine.

Ever since I signed the lease with Dr. Bollington, I've been the model tenant. I've never been late with rent. I shovel the sidewalks in winter. All I've done is bend to this man's will.

And I'm done.

"Yes, I'm in an unconventional relationship," I say through clenched teeth. "That doesn't give you the right to evict me. I'm an adult. I don't need your approval about how to live my life. If you insist on trying to evict me, I will hire a lawyer, and I will fight for my rights."

And I'll probably have to borrow money from Cassie again and eat Ramen noodles for the next five years. It doesn't matter. I'm done letting George Bollington bully me. This time, I'm going to stand up to him.

He sighs. "Before you continue, can I just say something? Dr. West and Dr. Long were already here this morning. We've made a deal. I'm not evicting you."

I stare at him, my heart beating in my chest. Oh no. Landon and Ben made a deal with my landlord? It's no secret that Dr. Bollington would love it if Landon and Ben shut their practice down. Surely that's not what he demanded in exchange.

They wouldn't give up their career for me, would they? Then I think of what they said to me last night. They promised to fix things for me. Surely they wouldn't go to such lengths?

If they can't be psychotherapists in town, they'll have to move. Leave New Summit, maybe head back to Manhattan. If they leave, what'll happen to us? If they asked, I'll close down my store and follow them in a heartbeat. If they want me.

Pivoting on my heel, I leave my landlord's office. My pulse races, my palms feel sticky with sweat. I have to find Landon and Ben. I have to talk them out of quitting. I can't let Bollington bully us. I won't let him win.

I almost run back to Ben's place. If Landon and Ben aren't there, I'm prepared to hunt through New Summit to find them. Fortunately for me, I run into them on my way back.

Coincidentally, we're outside China Garden again. This time, however, it's far too early for spring rolls. Maggie isn't even open yet.

"Tell me," I gasp, "that you didn't close your practice. Tell me that that's not the deal you made with my landlord. Please?"

Ben looks puzzled. "What are you talking about?"

"I just went to see Dr. Bollington. He said you made a deal with him." My voice rises with urgency. "He said he's not evicting me. He said you'd made a deal with him. What did he want?" As I speak, I'm searching their faces for signs of stress, but I don't find any. They look calm, relaxed. They don't look upset at all.

A tiny sliver of hope pierces the gloom of my heart. Landon smirks. "First you stood up for us to Amy, now you're concerned about our practice. It sounds like you care, Mia."

"Of course I care." Every single one of New Summit's five thousand, four hundred and thirty-five residents could surround the three of us right now, and I'd still say the words that are on my lips. "I'm in love with you."

Their expressions change in a flash, from teasing to serious. "Oh Mia," Ben mutters thickly, his eyes warm and tender, "I'm in love with you too."

"As am I." Landon folds me into his arms, and I fall readily into his embrace, pulling Ben into the hug too. I'm too happy to care who sees me. They're in love with me.

"You're not closing your practice? You're staying in town?" I whisper.

Landon nods. "And Bollington's going to remove the morality clause from your lease," he says. "He won't be bothering you anymore. Neither will Dennis," he adds darkly. "I warned him that I'd beat the snot out of him if he ever came anywhere near us."

"What?" I gape at the two of them. "He removed the morality clause? How?"

"You told us he was broke," Ben says. "I just used it against him. I threatened to tie him up in legal fees, then offered to pay if he'd remove the clause."

"First the stick, then the carrot," Landon grins. "Negotiating 101. And it totally worked."

"You offered to pay him? How much?" Curtains twitch on the street, and people stare out of their windows. At the rate I'm going, a Summit Star headline seems inevitable.

"It doesn't matter," Ben replies. "Mia, we love you, and in case you haven't noticed, we're not particularly hurting for money." He looks faintly embarrassed. "Our books sell well, and we don't need to see patients. We just do it because we love what we do."

Today's full of surprises. "You write books? Like sex therapy books? Really?"

"You didn't know?" Landon looks surprised. "You never Googled us?"

I shake my head at them fondly. "Seriously, you guys. It's New Summit. Why would I bother Googling you when you're the topic of conversation for the entire town?" I wince. "And now I am."

"Any regrets?"

I look into the eyes of the men I'm crazy about. "Not even a single one."

EPILOGUE

MIA

One year later...

Something's going on. Cassie and Nina have been acting mysterious all week. When I ask Sophia about it, she just giggles and tells me I'm imaging things.

We're in the midst of party planning. Sophia's turning eighteen in a couple of days. To my surprise, Landon's sister has elected to have a low-key potluck dinner. We're doing it in Ben's backyard because it's more spacious than Landon's.

"That smells good." Ben enters his kitchen, where I'm baking a lemon cake. I'm not much of a cook, but I like the precision of baking. Sophia's birthday cake will have three layers. Lemon, mango, and strawberry, held together with delicious icing and slices of fresh fruit.

I look ruefully around the room, which looks like it was at the epicenter of an icing sugar explosion. "Sorry about the mess," I say with a wince. Ben's a neat freak, and whenever he makes dinner, he cleans up as he goes along. "I promise I'll fix it when I'm done."

He chuckles. Coming up to me, he wraps his arms around my waist and nuzzles my neck. "Will you dress up as a maid when you do it?" he purrs into my ear.

My breath catches. "Naughty maid costumes are so cliché," I whisper. "You're not being very original, Dr. Long."

"No respect for the classics," he chides me, trailing warm kisses down the side of my neck.

My timer goes off, and I wriggle out of his grasp and open the oven door. "Where's Landon?" I ask, as I pull the cake pan out and let it cool on the wire rack.

"Picking up the tent and the chairs."

"Sweet." It's going to be a beautiful night. The dinner is planned for dusk. Hopefully, we'll eat under the stars, but the tent is a precaution in case it rains. I can't wait to see Ben's backyard, illuminated by strings of lights twined in the trees, the candlelit table covered with food, filled with our closest friends.

For about two months after the Chapman House Incident, as I like to call it, my ménage with Landon and Ben was the topic of gossip for all of New Summit. Thankfully, most people have moved on to other targets.

A couple of old ladies still look at me as if I'm leading the world into sin, but come on. Mrs. Fischer at the grocery store has a very boring life, as does Mrs. Marshall at the deli. If they want to continue to wonder about the exact logistics of three people in bed at once, more power to them. (Pro tip: Search the Internet.)

I made my decision to be with Landon and Ben. In the last year, I've never regretted it. Love is much more important than maintaining appearances.

As Landon and Ben promised, Dr. Bollington removed the morality clause on my lease. As a bonus, he stopped dropping into my store unannounced to bitch about Nina and Cassie. I'm not complaining. I hadn't realized how stressed out my landlord made me until he started avoiding me.

I'm dating Ben and Landon because I'm crazy about them. The added benefit of seeing less of Dr. Bollington? An unexpected perk.

Dennis is seeing someone else now; a woman called Sandra. She's new in town. I ran into the two of them having dinner at China Garden. Dennis was a dick to the waiter, and Sandra's eyes were glued to Dominic Zhang's butt. Good. The two of them deserve each other, and will undoubtedly make each other miserable.

It bothered me that Amy Cooke got off scot-free for her role in the Chapman Inn Incident. She'd been the biggest troublemaker of them all. But karma has a funny way of catching up with people. Amy was arrested two towns over for shoplifting. They let her off with a warning, but Tiffany Slater—yes, the same Tiffany who Dennis cheated on me with—saw it happen and came back and told the entire town. Amy's not enjoying being the target of New Summit gossip. Funny how that works.

"Is that lemon cake?" Landon walks in, looking hopefully at me. "That's my favorite. You didn't happen to make an extra one so we could eat it now, did you?"

I mock frown at him. "Don't you go near it," I warn him. "Remember what happened last time?"

Landon's lips curl into a grin at the memory. The last time I made a lemon cake, it was for Nina's birthday. I'd set it on the counter to cool, and Landon had cut himself a slice without realizing it was earmarked for a special occasion. I'd tried to salvage it, but the final product was worthy of being featured on Cake Wrecks. Good thing Nina has a sense of humor; she thought it was hilarious.

"Forget the lemon cake," Ben interjects with a wicked grin. "Mia's promised to wear a naughty maid costume and clean the kitchen."

Landon's eyes gleam with heat. "Has she?" he inquires silkily. He pulls a chair back and settles himself down on it. "This should be good."

"Ass."

They ignore that. "Take off your clothes, Mia," Ben orders smoothly. He eyes the baking-supply covered counter, then grabs a bottle of chocolate sauce and moves toward me with a gleam in his eyes.

Ooh. I wonder what he's planning. When Ben's wicked, he's very wicked.

I whip my t-shirt over my head and push my shorts down my hips. Unclasping my bra, I move my hands to my panties and remove them too.

"Very nice," Landon purrs in approval. "Come here, Mia. I want you to sit on my lap."

I move toward him, anticipation prickling at my skin. My nipples are hard pebbles, and my breasts ache to be touched, to be squeezed by them. My pussy feels slick with heat as I inch my way forward and settle myself on Landon's lap, my back against his chest, my thighs splayed wide open.

"You've made a mess of my kitchen, Mia." Ben's voice has a scolding note in it, though his eyes are amused. "It seems only fair that I reciprocate, don't you think?" He holds the chocolate sauce above me and squeezes the bottle.

The sauce drizzles down, falling on my breasts. As the drops fall, Ben's thumb rubs the chocolate, smearing it over my skin. My nipples tighten at the erotic sight of Ben's big hand on my chest, kneading my heavy breasts with his palms.

Then he bends his head down, and his mouth closes

over my nipples. His tongue licks the sauce off my skin, and my breathing catches. "Ben," I beg. "More, please."

Landon's hands grip the flesh of my thighs. He spreads me open even wider. "Keep your legs parted Mia," he instructs me sternly. His finger trails a path down my body, moving the sauce to my pussy. "Such a dirty girl," he teases. "Ben, what are we going to do with Mia?"

"I have a thought." Ben gets on his knees and pushes his head between my legs. He parts me with his thumbs, opening me to his gaze. His eyes feast on me. "Such a pretty pussy," he rasps out. His tongue teases me, toying with the opening of my slit, before sucking my clitoris into his mouth.

I bite my lip and grip Ben's dark hair in my fingers as he licks, nibbles, and sucks. My breathing comes in short bursts. Landon tweaks my nipples between his thumb and forefinger, smearing the chocolate all over.

"Suck," he orders, holding his fingers to my lips. "Clean me off, sweet Mia."

I open my mouth and lick the chocolate clean, groaning at the erotic heat of the moment. Ben's head between my legs, Landon's fingers on my nipples, it's all too much. My climax races toward me like a tidal wave. I'm drowning. Blood pounds in my ears. Every muscle in my body tenses and I feel the quiver in my belly. My pussy spasms and I flail. My thighs tighten, and it's only Ben's quick reflexes that keep his head from getting crushed by their grip.

"Wow," I exhale when I can think again. "I'm a complete mess." I wriggle on Landon's lap, feeling the thick outline of his cock press against my ass. "I think I should go shower."

I get up and stretch in an exaggeratedly languid motion. Ben's eyes are on me, heated and filled with lust. "Want to join me?"

They chuckle. "Well," Ben says, acting as if he's weighing his options, "I guess I should make sure you're clean."

Landon rises to his feet. "And I better double-check," he grins. "Let's go, Mia."

～

BEFORE I KNOW IT, it's the day of Sophia's party. The guests arrive. Cassie comes early to give us a hand with last-minute preparations. Nina shows up with her famous watermelon and feta cheese salad. Maggie Zhang arrives with spring rolls, and Ben has to stop me from intercepting her at the door and inhaling the entire dish.

Sophia arrives with a platter of chicken. "You didn't have to cook for your own party," I protest.

"I wanted to," she replies. I've been dying to make this lemon chicken recipe for a crowd." She hugs Ben, Landon, and I. "I invited a couple of co-workers. I hope that won't mess with the seating arrangements."

"The more, the merrier," Ben says easily.

Landon frowns suspiciously. "Who did you invite?" he asks. "I thought the only person you wanted at this party was Penny."

"I changed my mind," she replies. "Relax. Lucas and James are just co-workers."

Nina overhears us. "Oh, good, I'm glad you invited them," she says. "I feel bad for them. They just moved to New Summit and all they seem to do is work."

Before Landon can play protective big brother and demand more details, Sophia's friends arrive. Both men are tall and broad and are very definitely eye-candy. Cassie's eyes go wide when she sees them, and she grabs my elbow and drags me into a corner. "What are they doing here?" she whispers to me.

"You know them?"

"They come into my coffee shop every day," she replies. I look at her with interest. Her cheeks are flushed, and she won't meet my eyes. "I don't know their names. I call them Hottie One and Hottie Two."

"You didn't introduce yourself?" I raise my eyebrow. Cassie's never been shy. She's obviously interested; she keeps sneaking glances at the two of them. I grin at my best friend. "Somebody has a crush on Hottie One and Hottie Two," I sing-song.

"Stop that." She glares at me. "They're going to hear you."

I laugh and take pity on Cass. "Come on," I tell her. "Help me get the food on the table."

Five hours later, we've eaten food and cake and made our way through eight bottles of wine. When the clock strikes midnight, the party winds down. "As much as I'd love to stay," Nina says, getting to her feet, "It's been a long day, and I'm falling asleep." She gives Sophia a meaningful look. "Soph, you're opening the bar tomorrow morning, aren't you?"

Sophia shakes her head. "I think Mike's opening tomorrow," she corrects her boss before catching herself. "No, wait, what am I saying?" There's a twinkle in her eyes, and she gives Ben, Landon, and me a furtive look. "Of course I'm opening." She gets up. "I should get some sleep."

I frown at our guests. Everyone is suddenly in a hurry. I'm not sure what prompted the exodus, but I'm pretty sure it has to do with my feeling all week long that something's afoot.

"Cass?" I give my best friend a glare. "Stay a while longer, and we'll catch up?"

"Sorry Mia," she replies, keeping her gaze averted. "I've got to run."

"Where do you live, Cassie?" Hottie One asks. Okay, fine, his name isn't Hottie One, but it's such a good nickname for Lucas. "We can give you a ride home."

"I'm fine," she stammers. She looks a little trapped, and I grin inwardly. It's fun to see Cassie become tongue-tied when she's talking to a guy. It almost never happens. Ever since we were in high school, Cassie's had every guy in town wrapped around her little finger.

I think Lucas is interested in my friend, but I also think he's made of sterner stuff than the male population of New Summit. And the way James is looking at Cassie as well, as if she's a tasty morsel for him to devour? Whoa Nellie. Both of them? This is going to be very interesting.

Everyone clears out in a hurry. Ben and I walk them to the front door and watch as they walk down the street. "What was that about?" I ask him once people are out of earshot. "Why is everyone being so weird?"

"Come to the backyard again," he says.

I give him a narrowed look, then follow him.

The backyard is transformed.

The table has been cleared away. Rose petals are strewed on the cobblestone patio. Hurricane lamps dot the garden, casting a warm golden light over the place. Music plays softly through the speakers. And when Landon looks at me, the expression in his eyes makes me shiver.

My heart starts beating faster. "What's going on?" I ask them.

Landon takes a half-step toward me, the look on his face serious. "Mia," he says softly, "in the year we've been together, you've made me happier than I thought possible."

Ben nods solemnly, but doesn't speak. The expression in his eyes is enough. He's looking at me as if I was the most precious object in the world, and when I see his face, a lump forms in my throat.

"I'm the lucky one," I whisper. "Every day I spend with you, I feel blessed." I can feel my eyes tear up. "I'm so glad I walked into your office," I tell them in a half-laugh, half-sob. "Even if you chased me away by telling me you were going to watch me having sex with some random person."

Ben's lips curl up into a smile. From his pocket, he pulls out a chain. It's made of fine, filigreed gold, and it gleams in the candlelight. He reaches for my hand, turns it so my palm faces up, and drops the chain into it.

I lift it up and see what I missed. Dangling from the chain is a key. "Will you move in with us?" Ben asks.

I blink at him. "Here?" I ask, confused. I've dreamed of living with Ben and Landon many times during the year, but Landon can't move because he's Sophia's guardian, and unless the three of us can live together, there doesn't seem much point.

"Yes," Landon confirms. "Sophia's turned eighteen, and she's an adult now. She's old enough to live by herself." He smiles wryly. "Especially when I'm close enough to keep an eye on her."

That's why everyone was acting so strange. Sophia would have known Landon's plans. Cassie and Nina had to have been in on the plot too. I have no time to think of what I'm going to do to them because Ben's talking again.

"So, Mia," Ben says, his voice husky, "Will you live with us?"

Live with them. Wake up every morning in their bed,

sandwiched between their warm naked bodies. Have dinner together every evening. Squabble over the remote control. I can feel the smile break out on my face. "Yes," I squeal out, my fist closing around the key to Ben's house. "Of course I will."

I hug Landon and Ben tight. This is going to be amazing.

THANK YOU FOR READING MIA, Ben & Landon's story! I hope you love them as much as I do.

THE DIRTY SERIES

WANT MORE DIRTY? *Cassie's story - Dirty Talk - is next.* Read on for a free extended preview, or check out the other books in the DIRTY SERIES.

Dirty Therapy - Mia, Benjamin & Landon
Dirty Talk - Cassie, James & Lucas
Dirty Games - Nina, Scott & Zane
Dirty Words - Maggie, Lars & Ethan

Or, buy the collection for a discount...
Dirty - the Complete Collection

DO YOU ENJOY FUN, light, contemporary romances with lots of heat and humor? Want to read *Boyfriend by the Hour (A Romantic Comedy)* for free? Want to stay up-to-date on new releases, freebies, sales, and more? (There will be an occasional cat picture.) **Sign up to my newsletter!** You'll get the book right away, and unless I have a very important announcement—like a new release—I only email once a week.

A PREVIEW OF DIRTY TALK

Cassie:

It's Monday morning. The hottest two guys in New Summit are in my coffee shop. Sounds pretty good, right?

Wrong.

Because these aren't just any guys. Nope. I'm serving coffee and muffins to James Fowler and Lucas Bennett. Sex vloggers, YouTube stars, and hosts of the no-holds-barred show about blowjobs, bondage, and buttsex.

Yup. Ladies and gentlemen, I'm crushing on the hosts of Dirty Talk. Somebody kill me now.

The doorbell chimes and I look up, automatically pasting a smile on my face, one that fades when I see that it's my landlord, Dr. George Bollington, psychotherapist and all around pain in the ass. Ever since Mia started dating Landon and Ben, the crotchety old man has switched his attention to me. If Mia weren't my best friend, I'd strangle her.

"Hello, Dr. Bollington," I chirp. "Can I interest you in a

scone this morning? On the house, of course." Hey, I'm not above bribery. The last time Bollington was here, he went on an epic rant about the subdivisions they're building on the outskirts of town. His tirade lasted twenty-one minutes.

That would have been bad enough, but it got worse. Matthew Steadman, the foreman in charge of building the gated community, had been in my coffee shop at that time, and he'd overheard. He didn't say anything to Bollington— Matthew's far too classy to start a fight—but he'd left and hasn't been back since, and neither has any of his crew.

My landlord surveys the offerings behind the glass cabinet with a frown. "You have any of those carrot muffins?"

Just one. *Forgive me, Mia. I know they're your favorite, but I'll sacrifice my first-born to get Bollington out of here.* "I do," I reply brightly, putting it on a white ceramic plate and handing it to him. "Coffee with that?"

"A large, please." Bollington sets the muffin down on the wooden communal table that fills the front area of Cassie's Coffee. Belatedly, I curse myself for my stupidity. I should have put the muffin in a paper bag for him, not on a plate. *Do you want him to stay the whole day, Cass?*

Out of the corner of my eye, I can see Lucas trying to stifle his chuckles. *Jerk,* I mouth silently to him. Lucas knows perfectly well that I'm trying to get rid of my landlord, and he's clearly amused by my inability to do so.

James is sitting next to Lucas on the battered leather couch, his laptop resting on his knees. He looks up and takes in the situation with a grin. Shaking his head, he rises to his feet and walks over toward us. "Dr. Bollington," he greets the older man heartily. "You're just the person I wanted to run into today."

As if.

"You did?" My landlord looks suspicious.

"Indeed." James extends his hand in greeting. "My name is James Fowler," he says. "You might not know me, but I just moved here."

Inwardly, I snort. Of course Dr. Bollington knows who Lucas and James are; he's a gossipy old man who is intensely interested in anyone who moves into town. His head will probably explode when the new subdivision is built and hundreds of strangers invade New Summit.

Dr. Bollington shakes James' hand, his expression stiff. I'm convinced he disapproves of everyone under forty on principle. "How can I help you?"

"My father had a stroke back in February," James replies. "He's undergoing rehab now, but it's hard for him. He has to relearn so much, and he gets frustrated. I thought that if he talked it out with a professional..."

Bollington's eyes light up at the prospect of a new patient. "Of course." He pats James' back. "That's an excellent idea."

James gives me a sidelong wink. "Would you mind if I walk back with you to your office and book an appointment?" he asks the therapist.

"Yes, yes, certainly. Cassie, I'll need my coffee and muffin to go."

I hurry to do what my landlord asks. *Thank you,* I whisper to James, then watch the two of them walk out of the door, James' dark head bent as he listens to something Bollington is saying.

"Admit it, Cassie." Lucas has walked up to the counter, and he's standing in front of me, his hazel eyes twinkling and a smug grin on his face. "I'm not really that much of a jerk."

"James was the one who rescued me from Bollington," I point out, though I can't stop the answering grin from breaking out across my face. "Is it true, what James was saying? His dad had a stroke?"

Lucas' smile dims. "Yeah," he confirms. "Patrick isn't doing too well."

"I've never seen him in here, have I?"

"No." Lucas runs his hand through his hair. "He's pretty depressed, and he doesn't leave the house much. James is having a rough time of it."

I do some math in my head. "You moved here two months ago," I ask, a question in my voice. "Because of the stroke?"

Lucas raises an eyebrow at my unexpected chattiness, and I blush. Ever since the two of them walked me home after Sophia's birthday party three weeks ago, I've been keeping them at arm's length.

That night, they'd been flirting with me, and I'd reciprocated. Then I got home and Googled them. Once I found out about Dirty Talk, I knew I couldn't get involved with them. They live their lives in front of the camera, and I have too many demons to risk exposure.

"Yeah," Lucas replies, satisfying my curiosity readily. "His health insurance didn't cover all his bills, and he ate through his savings while in the hospital. This place is a lot cheaper than Manhattan."

"So James moved in with his father to help out, and you did too? You guys bought that wreck on Baker Street, didn't you?" I've classified James and Lucas as bad boys because of Lucas' tattoos and the raunchiness of their show, but now I reassess my first impression. There's more to these guys than meets the eye.

"It's going to take us a few more months to get used to how everyone knows everything in this town," Lucas mutters ruefully. "Yeah, Patrick needed our help." He shrugs. "It's no big deal. It's just what you do for family, you know?"

There's a pang in my heart. My own relationship with my parents was much rockier. "I don't know," I reply. "My mom and dad are dead."

An expression of sympathy flits across his face. "I'm sorry, Cass," he says quietly.

"Don't worry about it." I try for a flippant tone, but judging from the watchful expression on Lucas' face, I don't manage to pull it off. "It was almost nine years ago. They died in a car crash."

I don't add that if they hadn't been killed in the accident, we'd probably be estranged. My parents—especially my mother—weren't interested in me if I wasn't performing. When I was winning every beauty pageant in the country as a toddler, they approved of me and showered me with presents. When I started rebelling, they were less kind. "Stop shoving food in your face," my mother used to say to me every time I sat down for a meal. "No one will find you attractive if you get fat."

Here's a parenting tip, mom. When your daughter is seven, don't tell her she eats like a pig.

"Cass?" Lucas' voice interrupts my reverie. "Are you okay?"

I pull my attention back to the hunk in front of me. God, he's gorgeous. His black Metallica t-shirt hugs his broad chest. His faded jeans stretch across his crotch, and I want to grab his butt and lick every available inch of him. And if James happens to be watching... *well, that's even better.*

Unfortunately, there's my camera phobia. After a childhood of being made up to look like a doll and being leered at by old men, I'm done with the spotlight.

James walks back into the coffee shop. "You owe me," he says with a grin. "That man loves the sound of his own voice. I couldn't get a word in edgewise."

"Sorry," I say ruefully. "Can I offer you a muffin on the house for your help?"

"A muffin?" James shakes his head, looking indignant. "I put myself through fifteen minutes of hell for a muffin? I don't think so, Cass." His lips quirk into a smile. "Have dinner with me."

I wish I could. I really do. It's not the first time I've turned one of them down. They asked me out the night of Sophia's party, and I declined then as well. "Sorry," I say, keeping my voice light, "the muffin's the best I can do."

Lucas gives me a searching look. "You won't have dinner with James," he says. "You won't have dinner with me. Will you have dinner with both of us?"

You know what this moment feels like? Like I'm on a diet, and someone's offering me two deliciously glazed donuts. And they're right there, tempting me, calling to me, whispering that a little sin won't matter...

"I can't."

"Well, it was worth a shot." James smiles easily at me, unperturbed at my refusal. Why would he be? He's a YouTube star. I've read the comments section of their channel. Women throw themselves at Lucas and James shamelessly, offering to do anything for a little *Dirty Talk* of their own. I'm fairly sure that the only reason James and Lucas are interested in me is because I said '*No*'. It's not a word they hear a lot.

They move back to their seats on the couch. Lucas pulls his laptop toward him and starts typing something on it. James ignores his computer and fiddles with his phone, and I get back to the grind of making coffee and serving customers.

Two hours later, the morning rush has almost died down when the door opens once again. I look up with a smile pasted on my face, and my heart skips a beat when I realize who's just walked in.

It's Stuart Sutherland.

High school quarterback, prom king, and the most popular guy in our high school, Stuart Sutherland was a symbol of everything I thought I wanted from life when I was a teenager. I was the kid whose mom made her participate in beauty pageants. *Trailer trash,* people would sneer behind my back. *Desperate for attention,* other people would say sadly. Not that anyone ever interfered, of course. That just wasn't done in New Summit.

Stuart, on the other hand, had everything. His mother was the head of the PTA. His dad owned the biggest boat in the marina. He lived in the mansion on the hill, and when he turned sixteen, his parents bought him a red Corvette.

After high school, Stuart got recruited by Ohio State to play football, and he even made it to a practice team in the NFL. He lives in California now and only comes back to New Summit for the holidays.

My pulse is racing. It's stupid and childish, but I had the biggest crush on him in high school. He never even noticed me, but God, I pined so hard for him. When I was fifteen, I would have sacrificed my first-born child if it would make Stuart Sutherland *notice* me.

I have no idea what he's doing at Cassie's Coffee.

"Cassie Turner." Stuart flashes me a grin as he struts into the room. "It's been eight years since I last saw you, hasn't it?"

My mouth falls open. Stuart Sutherland knows my name? Teenage-Cassie is doing a happy dance. Come to think of it, from the way my heart is hammering in my chest, Adult-Cassie is having a similar reaction.

"Hey Stuart," I reply. *Be cool Cassie, be cool.* "I didn't know you were in town."

"Yeah, I'm moving back," he replies, his gaze darting around my little space. What he thinks of the exposed brick walls, the high ceilings, and the warm lighting, I have no idea, because I don't register his next words. I'm still stuck on the *'I'm moving back'* bombshell.

Stuart Sutherland is back in town? Things are looking up.

"I'm going to work for my dad," he adds. He pulls his wallet out of his back pocket. "Can I get a cup of coffee to go, please?"

"Of course." I hurry to fill his order, surreptitiously wiping my sweaty palms on my apron. *Get a grip,* I scold myself.

"Thanks," he says, taking the cup I hand him. "By the way, Cassie, you want to go out Friday night? Maybe we can stop by at the bar down the street?"

Stuart Sutherland just asked me out. Ladies and gentlemen, it's time for confetti and streamers.

"Yes," I choke out. "That'd be great."

"Perfect." He pulls a business card out of his wallet and pushes it toward me. "Call me on Wednesday, and we'll work out the details." Scooping up the change from his five dollar bill, he winks at me and leaves.

Out of the corner of my eye, I can see James and Lucas watching the entire interaction, identical frowns of disapproval on their faces. *I don't care,* I tell myself defiantly. *I can go out with whoever I want.*

Yet, I can't meet their eyes.

CLICK **here to keep reading Dirty Talk - Cassie's story!**

ABOUT TARA CRESCENT

Get a free story from Tara when you sign up to Tara's mailing list.

Tara Crescent writes steamy contemporary romances for readers who like hot, dominant heroes and strong, sassy heroines.

When she's not writing, she can be found curled up on a couch with a good book, often with a cat on her lap.

She lives in Toronto.

Tara also writes sci-fi romance as Lili Zander. Check her books out at http://www.lilizander.com

Find Tara on:
www.taracrescent.com
taracrescent@gmail.com

ALSO BY TARA CRESCENT

MÉNAGE ROMANCE

Club Ménage

Claiming Fifi

Taming Avery

Keeping Kiera - *coming soon*

Ménage in Manhattan

The Bet

The Heat

The Wager

The Hack

The Dirty Series

Dirty Therapy

Dirty Talk

Dirty Games

Dirty Words

The Cocky Series

Her Cocky Doctors

Her Cocky Firemen

Standalone Books

Dirty X6

CONTEMPORARY ROMANCE

The Drake Family Series

Temporary Wife (A Billionaire Fake Marriage Romance)

Fake Fiance (A Billionaire Second Chance Romance)

Standalone Books

Hard Wood

MAX: A Friends to Lovers Romance

A Touch of Blackmail

A Very Paisley Christmas

Boyfriend by the Hour

BDSM ROMANCE

Assassin's Revenge

Nights in Venice

Mr. Banks (A British Billionaire Romance)

Teaching Maya

The House of Pain

The Professor's Pet

The Audition

The Watcher

Doctor Dom

Dominant - *A Boxed Set containing The House of Pain, The Professor's Pet, The Audition and The Watcher*

~

You can also keep track of my new releases by signing up for my mailing list!

Made in the USA
Middletown, DE
23 June 2021